THE CASE OF THE BORROWED BRUNETTE
THE CASE OF THE BURIED CLOCK
THE CASE OF THE FOOTLOOSE DOLL
THE CASE OF THE LAZY LOVER
THE CASE OF THE SHOPLIFTER'S SHOE
THE CASE OF THE FABULOUS FAKE
THE CASE OF THE CROOKED CANDLE
THE CASE OF THE HOWLING DOG
THE CASE OF THE FIERY FINGERS
THE CASE OF THE HAUNTED HUSBAND
THE CASE OF THE MYTHICAL MONKEYS
THE CASE OF THE SHAPELY SHADOW
THE CASE OF THE GLAMOROUS GHOST
THE CASE OF THE GRINNING GORILLA
THE CASE OF THE NEGLIGENT NYMPH
THE CASE OF THE PERJURED PARROT
THE CASE OF THE RESTLESS REDHEAD
THE CASE OF THE SUNBATHER'S DIARY
THE CASE OF THE VAGABOND VIRGIN
THE CASE OF THE DEADLY TOY
THE CASE OF THE DUBIOUS BRIDEGROOM
THE CASE OF THE LONELY HEIRESS
THE CASE OF THE EMPTY TIN
THE CASE OF THE GOLDDIGGER'S PURSE
THE CASE OF THE LAME CANARY
THE CASE OF THE BLACK-EYED BLOND
THE CASE OF THE CARETAKER'S CAT
THE CASE OF THE GILDED LILY
THE CASE OF THE ROLLING BONES
THE CASE OF THE SILENT PARTNER
THE CASE OF THE VELVET CLAWS
THE CASE OF THE BAITED HOOK
THE CASE OF THE COUNTERFEIT EYE
THE CASE OF THE PHANTOM FORTUNE
THE CASE OF THE WORRIED WAITRESS
THE CASE OF THE CALENDAR GIRL
THE CASE OF THE TERRIFIED TYPIST
THE CASE OF THE CAUTIOUS COQUETTE
THE CASE OF THE SPURIOUS SPINSTER
THE CASE OF THE DUPLICATE DAUGHTER

The Case of the
Stuttering Bishop

Erle Stanley Gardner

BALLANTINE BOOKS • NEW YORK

ISBN 0-345-35680-2

This edition published by arrangement with William Morrow and Company, Inc.

Manufactured in the United States of America

First Ballantine Books Edition: December 1988

Chapter 1

Perry Mason's eyes came to a hard focus on the figure which paused uncertainly in the doorway of his private office. "Come in, Bishop," he said.

The stocky figure, clad in loose-fitting black broadcloth, bowed slightly and strode toward the chair which Mason indicated. Above the white expanse of the ecclesiastical collar, a sun-burned face set off the cool gray of glinting eyes. The short, sturdy legs, terminating in well-worn black shoes, marched briskly enough, but, watching the man, Mason knew those legs would have marched just as steadily had they been propelling the rugged torso toward the electric chair.

The bishop sat down and turned to face the lawyer.

"Cigarette?" Mason asked, pushing a case toward his visitor.

The bishop reached toward the cigarettes, then paused and said, "I've been smoking them for an hour. Two puffs and I'm f-f-finished." As his lips stumbled over the first syllable of the last word, the bishop lapsed into abrupt silence for the space of two deep breaths, as though trying to control himself. After a moment, he said, his voice firm as the fingers of a pianist which, having fumbled, atone for the slip by an added emphasis, "If you don't mind, I'd like to light up my pipe."

"Not at all," Mason said, and noticed that the stubby pipe which the man produced from his left pocket was somehow very like the man himself.

"My secretary tells me you're Bishop William Mallory, of Sydney, Australia, and you want to see me about a manslaughter case," the lawyer said, breaking the ice for his visitor.

Bishop Mallory nodded, took a leather pouch from his pocket, stuffed fragrant grains of tobacco into the encrusted bowl of the polished briar, clamped his teeth firmly on the

1

curved stem and struck a match. Watching him, Mason couldn't tell whether he cupped the match in both hands to keep his fingers from shaking, or from a mechanical habit of shielding a match against the wind.

As the flickering flame illuminated the high forehead, the somewhat flat face with its high cheekbones and determined jaw, Mason's eyes narrowed into thoughtful scrutiny. "Go ahead," he said.

Bishop Mallory puffed out several little clouds of smoke. He wasn't the sort of man who would squirm uneasily in a chair, but his manner gave every indication of mental uneasiness. "I'm afraid," Bishop Mallory said, "that my legal education is a little rusty, but I'd like to know about the limitations of a m-m-manslaughter case."

As he stuttered for the second time, his teeth clamped firmly on the pipe stem, and the rapidity with which he puffed out little spurts of smoke bore evidence both of his nervousness and of his irritation at the defect in his speech.

Mason said slowly, "We have, in this state, what is known as a statute of limitations. All felonies, other than murder and the embezzlement of public money, or the falsification of public records, must be prosecuted within three years after the crime has been committed."

"Suppose the person who committed the crime can't be found?" Bishop Mallory asked, and his gray eyes peered eagerly at the lawyer through the blue haze of tobacco smoke.

"If the defendant's out of the state," Mason said, "the time during which he is absent from the state isn't counted."

The bishop hastily averted his eyes, but not in time to avoid the expression of disappointment which clouded them.

Mason went on talking smoothly and easily, after the manner of a doctor who seeks to set the mind of a patient at ease before an operation. "You see, it's difficult for a defendant to secure evidence in his own behalf after a period of years, just as it's difficult for the prosecution to get the evidence of witnesses to a stale crime. For that reason, in all crimes, save those of the greatest importance, the law fixes this limitation. That's the legal limitation, but there's a practical limitation as well. Therefore, even if a district attorney technically is permitted to

2

prosecute a crime, he might hesitate to do so after the lapse of several years."

During the ensuing moment of silence, the bishop seemed to be groping in his mind for the proper words with which to clothe an idea. The lawyer brought matters to a head by laughing and saying, "After all, Bishop, a client consulting an attorney is somewhat in the position of a patient consulting a doctor. Suppose you tell me just what's on your mind, instead of beating around the bush with abstract questions."

Bishop Mallory said eagerly, "Do you mean that if a crime had been committed twenty-two years ago, a district attorney wouldn't p-p-prosecute, even if the defendant hadn't been in the state?" And this time, so eager was he to hear the answer to his question that he showed no embarrassment at the impediment which manifested itself in his speech.

"What you would consider manslaughter," Mason said, "*might* be considered murder by a district attorney."

"No, this is manslaughter. A warrant of arrest was issued, but was never served because the person skipped out."

"What were the circumstances?" Mason asked.

"A person was driving an automobile and struck another car. The claim was made that she . . . this p-p-person . . . was drunk."

"Twenty-two years ago?" Mason exclaimed.

The bishop nodded.

"There weren't many of those cases twenty-two years ago," Mason observed, studying his visitor's features.

"I know that," the bishop agreed, "but this was in one of the outlying counties where a district attorney was . . . overly zealous."

"What do you mean by that?" Mason asked.

"I mean that he tried to take advantage of every technicality the law offered."

Mason nodded and said, "Were you, by any chance, the defendant, Bishop?"

The look of surprise on the bishop's face was unmistakably genuine. "I was in Australia at the time," he said.

"Twenty-two years," Mason said, watching the bishop with thought-slitted eyes, "is a long time, even for a zealous district

3

attorney. What's more, district attorneys come, and district attorneys go. There have probably been quite a few changes in the political set-up of that county during the last twenty-two years."

The bishop nodded absently, as though political changes had but little to do with the question under discussion.

"Therefore," Mason said, "since you are still concerned about the case, I gather there's more behind it than an over-zealous district attorney."

Bishop Mallory's eyes snapped wide open. He stared at Mason and then said, "You're a very c-c-c-clever lawyer, Mr. Mason."

Mason waited several silent seconds before saying, "Suppose you tell me the rest of it, Bishop."

Bishop Mallory puffed at his pipe, then said abruptly, "Do you take cases on a contingency basis?"

"Yes, sometimes."

"Would you fight for a poor person against a millionaire?"

Mason said grimly, "I'd fight for a client against the devil himself."

The bishop smoked in meditative silence for several seconds, apparently trying to find just the right method of approach. Then he cupped the warm bowl of the pipe in his hand and said, "Do you know a Renwold C. Brownley?"

"I know of him," Mason said.

"Have you ever done any work for him . . . I mean, are you his lawyer?"

"No."

Bishop Mallory said, "You're going to be consulted about a case against Renwold Brownley. There's a great deal of money involved. I don't know how much, perhaps a million, perhaps more. You will have to fight the case from scratch. If you win it, you can get a large fee, two or three hundred thousand dollars. I warn you that Brownley is going to be hard to h-h-h-handle. It's going to be a mean case. You'll be protecting the rights of a woman who has been greatly wronged. And the only chance you stand of winning the case is through my testimony as a witness."

4

Mason's eyes became hard and cautious. "So what?" he asked.

Bishop Mallory shook his head. "Don't misunderstand me," he said. "*I'm* not asking for anything. I don't want anything for myself. I *do* want to see justice done. Now, if I'm to be the main witness in the case, it would weaken the value of my testimony if it appeared I had taken a preliminary partisan interest, would it not?"

"It might," Mason admitted.

The bishop pushed the curved stem of his pipe between his lips, tamped the tobacco in the bowl with the tip of a stubby forefinger, nodded his head thoughtfully and said, "That's the way I felt about it." Mason sat in watchful silence. "So," Bishop Mallory went on, "I don't want anyone to know I have been here. Naturally, I wouldn't lie about it. If, when I get on the witness stand, they should ask me questions about having taken an interest in the case, I'd answer those questions truthfully, but it would be better for all concerned if those questions weren't asked.

"Now, I'm going to call you in about an hour. At that time I'll tell you where to come to meet me and I'll introduce you to the persons who are vitally interested. Their stories will sound incredible, but will be true. It's a case of a very rich man having been very ruthless and very unjust.

"After that interview," Bishop Mallory went on, "I must disappear and have no further contact with you until you find me and drag me into court as a witness. And, you'll have to be very clever to find me, Mr. Mason. But I think I can count on you for that." The bishop nodded to himself as though entirely satisfied with the situation. He got to his feet abruptly, and his short, stubby legs pounded across the office. He opened the exit door into the corridor, turned, bowed to Mason, and slammed the door behind him.

Della Street, Mason's secretary, emerged from the inner office where she had been taking notes, and said, "How do you figure that one, Chief?"

Mason, standing in the center of his office, feet spread apart, hands thrust deep in his trousers pockets, stared intently at the carpet with eyes which were held in fixed focus. "I'll be damned if I know," he said slowly.

"How did you size him up?" she asked.

"If he's a bishop," Mason said, "he's pretty human, no stiffness to his broadcloth, a stubby pipe and the general atmosphere of being a broad-minded man-of-the-world. Notice that he said he wouldn't lie if the other side asked him certain questions, but that it was up to me to keep them from asking those questions."

"Why do you say, *if* he's a bishop?" Della Street asked.

Mason said slowly, "Bishops don't stutter."

"What do you mean?"

"Bishops," he said, "have to work up. They're men who must be of outstanding ability and they have to talk in public. Now, if a person stuttered, he'd hardly become a minister, any more than he would a lawyer. But, if he *did* stutter and *was* a minister, he'd hardly become a bishop."

"I see," she said. "So you think . . ." She became silent as she stared at him with wide, startled eyes.

He nodded slowly and said, "The man may be a damn clever imposter. On the other hand, he may be a bishop who's been through some experience which has produced an emotional shock. If I remember my medical jurisprudence, one of the causes of stuttering in adults is a sudden emotional shock."

Della Street's voice showed concern. "Listen, Chief," she said, "if you're going to take this man's word for something and start fighting a multimillionaire like Renwold C. Brownley, you'd first better find out whether he's a genuine bishop or an imposter. It might make quite a difference."

Mason nodded slowly and said, "That was exactly what I had in mind. Ring up the Drake Detective Agency and tell Paul Drake to drop whatever he's doing and come to my office at once."

Chapter 2

Paul Drake, head of the Drake Detective Agency, slid sidewise into the big overstuffed leather chair, his back propped against one of the chair arms, his legs draped over the other. He regarded Perry Mason with protruding, somewhat glassy eyes which peered in expressionless appraisal from his rather florid face. When his facial muscles were relaxed, his mouth had a peculiar carp-like appearance which gave him a look of droll humor. He looked so utterly unlike a detective that he was able to accomplish startling results.

Perry Mason, pacing back and forth across his office, thumbs hooked in the armholes of his vest, tossed words over his shoulder. "A Church of England bishop who claims to be William Mallory from Sydney, Australia, has consulted me. He's a close-mouthed chap with the face of an outdoor man. . . . You know what I mean, the skin tanned as though accustomed to the bite of wind. . . . I don't know when he arrived. He wants to know about a manslaughter case growing out of drunken driving in an outlying county twenty-two years ago."

"What does he look like?" the detective asked.

"About fifty-three or fifty-five, five foot six or seven, weight one hundred eighty, wears the ecclesiastical broadcloth and collar, smokes a pipe by preference, cigarettes on occasion, gray eyes, hair darkish and thick but gray around the temples, a competent sort of an individual, stutters occasionally."

"Stutters?" Drake asked.

"That's right."

"You mean he's a bishop and he stutters?"

"Yes."

"Bishops don't stutter, Perry."

"That's just the point," Mason said. "This stuttering must

be a recent development, probably due to some emotional shock. I want to find out what that emotional shock is."

"How did he take the stuttering?" Drake asked. "What I mean is, how did he act when he stuttered?"

"Acted just like a golfer does when he tops a drive or misses a mashie."

"I don't like it, Perry," the detective said. "He sounds like a phoney to me. How do you know he's a bishop? Are you just taking his word for it?"

"That's right," Mason agreed readily enough.

"You'd better let me check on him and get all the dope."

"That's exactly what I want you to do, Paul. The bishop is going to get in touch with me in an hour. Shortly after that I've got to say yes or no to a case involving a lot of money. If the bishop's on the square, I'll be inclined to say yes. If he's a phoney I want to say no."

"What's the case?" Drake asked.

"This," Mason told him, "is in the strictist confidence. It involves Renwold C. Brownley, and if there's anything to it at all, it may carry a fee running into the hundreds of thousands." The detective gave a low whistle. "It involves, among other things, an old manslaughter charge, growing out of drunken driving."

"How old?" Drake asked.

"Twenty-two years, Paul."

The detective raised his eyebrows.

"Now there weren't many drunken driving cases twenty-two years ago. Moreover, this case was in an outlying county. I want to know about it, and I want to know about it right away. Put a bunch of men to work. Cover Orange County, San Bernardino, Riverside, Kern and Ventura. I think the defendant was a woman. Check through the records and see if there's an old manslaughter case dating back to 1914 where a woman was the defendant—a case which has never been cleaned up.

"Cable your correspondents in Sydney, Australia, to find out all about Bishop William Mallory. Cover the steamship records, find out when Bishop Mallory arrived in California and what he's been doing with his time since then. Cover the principal hotels and see if they have a Bishop Mallory registered. Put just as many men on the case as you need, but get me results, and get them fast. I want action!"

Drake sighed lugubriously and said, "I'll say you want action! You want a week's work done in sixty minutes."

Mason made no answer, but went on as though he had not heard the comment. "I'm particularly anxious to find out whom he's contacting. Get a line on him as quickly as possible, shadow everyone who comes in contact with him."

The detective slid his back down until only his hip pockets were resting on the polished leather surface of the chair. Then he spun around, lurched to his feet and straightened his long legs and neck, squaring shoulders which were inclined to slump slightly forward. "Okay, Perry," he said, "I'm on my way."

At the corridor door the detective turned and said to Mason, "Suppose I find out this fellow is a phoney, are you going to show him up?"

"Not me," Mason said, grinning. "I'll string him along and see what's back of the impersonation."

"Bet you even money he's a phoney," Drake said.

"His face looks honest," Mason asserted.

"Most bunco men's do," Drake told him. "That's why they make good in the racket."

"Well," Mason said dryly, "it's not *too* highly improbable that a real bishop should have an honest face. Get the hell out of here and get to work."

Drake stood still in the doorway. "You're not taking my bet, eh, Perry?" Mason reached quickly for a law book, as though intending to use it as a missle, and the detective hastily slammed the door shut.

The telephone rang. Mason answered it and heard Della Street's voice saying, "Chief, there's a taxi driver out here. I think I'd better bring him in and let him talk to you."

"A taxi driver?"

"Yes."

"What the devil does *he* want?"

"Money," she said.

"And you think *I* should see him?"

"Yes."

"Can you tell me what it's about over the telephone?"

"I don't think I'd better."

"You mean he's where he can hear what you're saying?"

"Yes."

Mason said, "Okay, bring him in." He had hardly hung up the telephone receiver when the door from the outer office opened, and Della Street ushered an apologetic but insistent cab driver into the office.

"This man drove Bishop Mallory to the office, Chief," she said.

The cab driver nodded and said, "He asked me to wait out in front of the building. I'm in a loading zone and a cop boots me out. I find a parking place and roost there and don't see anything of my man. My meter's clocking up time, so I asked the elevator starter. It happens the starter remembers him. He says the guy asked for your office, so here I am. He's a stocky chap with a turned-round collar, around fifty or fifty-five."

Mason's voice showed no interest. "He hasn't left the building?"

"I haven't seen him come out and I've been watching, and the elevator starter says he hasn't come out because he remembered him. I've got three eighty-five on my meter and I wanna know where it's coming from."

"Where'd you pick this chap up?" Mason asked. The cab driver hesitated. Mason pulled a roll of bills from his pocket, pulled off a five and said with a grin, "I just wanted to protect myself by getting the information before advancing the money to cover the cab bill."

The cab driver said, "I picked him up at the Regal Hotel."

"And drove him directly here?"

"That's right."

"Was he in a hurry?"

"Plenty."

Mason passed over the bill and said, "I don't think there's any use waiting any longer."

"Not the way that cop's bawling me out, there isn't," the driver said, handing Mason the change, "and I just want to say this is damn white of you, governor. I've heard of you from the boys. You're a square shooter who gives a working man the

10

breaks. If there's ever anything *I* can do for *you*, don't hesitate to say so. The name's Winters, Jack Winters."

"Fine, Jack," Mason said. "Perhaps someday I'll get you on a jury, and in the meantime your fare would doubtless give you a tip, so keep the change and buy yourself a cigar."

The man made a grinning exit.

Mason picked up the telephone, called Paul Drake and said, "Paul, start your men working on the Regal Hotel. He may be registered there as William Mallory. Call me back just as soon as you get him located, and be sure to tail everyone who contacts him."

Della Street, a model of slim efficiency in a close-fitting gray tailored suit, said, "Jackson would like to talk with you about the traction case, if you can spare a minute."

Mason nodded and said, "Send him in."

A moment later he was closeted with his law clerk, outlining the position which the respondent should take on an appeal from a large verdict in a personal injury case. From time to time, Della Street came and went, bustling about the office, cleaning up odds and ends of routine matters, as she always did before Mason became absorbed in an important case which was destined to occupy all of his time.

Mason was pointing out to his clerk the fallacy of the position assumed by the appellant in its opening brief, when Della Street entered the office to say, "Paul Drake on the line, Chief. He says it's important."

Mason nodded, picked up the telephone and heard Drake's voice speaking rapidly, with the drawl completely absent: "Perry, I'm over at the Regal Hotel, and I think you'd better come over right away if you're interested in that bishop of yours."

"Coming right now," Mason said, reaching for his hat as he hung up the telephone. "You needn't stay, Della," he told her, looking at his watch. "I'll call you at your apartment if there's anything I want. Jackson, go ahead and work out the brief along those lines and let me look it over before you file it." He rushed out into the corridor and caught a cab at the curb in front of the building. It took him less than fifteen minutes to reach the Regal Hotel, where Drake was waiting in the lobby,

11

accompanied by a thick-necked, bald-headed individual with sneering eyes, who held the soggy end of a black cigar clamped between thick, pendulous lips.

"Shake hands with Jim Pauley, the house detective here," Drake said to Perry Mason.

Pauley said, "Howdydo, Mason," and shook hands, his eyes seeming to take a professional interest in Mason's features.

"Pauley's an old pal of mine," Drake said, closing one of his eyes in a slowly surreptitious wink, "one of the ablest detectives in the game. I tried to hire him a couple of times but didn't have money enough. He's got a level head on his shoulders and has given me several tips that have worked out. He's a good man to remember, Perry. He might help you a lot sometime with some of *your* cases."

Pauley shifted the cigar and said deprecatingly, "Aw, I ain't no genius. I just use common sense."

Drake's hand rested on the house detective's shoulder. "That's the way he is, Perry—modest. You'd never think he was the chap that caught the Easops, the slickest bunch of passkey thieves that ever worked the hotels. Of course, the police took all the credit, but it was Jim here who really did the job. . . . Well, we've uncovered something, Perry—that is, Jim has. I guess you'd better tell him, Jim."

The house detective raised thick fingers to pull the soggy cigar from his mouth, as he said importantly, lowering his voice and looking about him as though fearful lest he should be overheard: "You know, we've got a William Mallory staying here and he's a queer one. He left here to go someplace in a taxi, and I noticed someone was tailing him in another cab. An ordinary man wouldn't have noticed it, but that's my business. I'm trained to that stuff, and I spotted the guy in a minute when he pulled away from the curb. I seen him speak to his driver and nod toward the cab Mallory was riding in, and I didn't need to hear what was said. He could just as well have put it in writing for me, so I sort of made up my mind I'd keep an eye on this guy, Mallory, because his tail might be anything from a private dick to a G-man. We're running a nice hotel here, gents, and we don't want the class of trade that carries a tail. So

12

I decided I'd have a talk with this chap when he got back, and tell him we wanted his room.

"Well, when he came back there was a red-headed dame sitting in the lobby. She got up as soon as she got her lamps on him and flashed him the high-sign. He gave her a half a nod and then went right to the elevator. He has a funny way of walking. His legs are short, and he just pounds along with 'em at a mile-a-minute clip.

"Well, gents, I figured that this dame in the lobby was waiting for him and he wouldn't be up in his room more than five minutes before she'd join him. Now, it ain't easy to argue with a guest and tell him you want his room. Sometimes they get rough and threaten lawsuits. Most of the times it's a bluff, but it's a lot of trouble just the same. So I figured it would be a lot easier to let this jane go up to the room, and then spring it on this bird—you know what I mean."

Mason nodded, and Drake said, in a voice which was a soothing murmur, "I told you he was smart, Perry. *Plenty* smart! That's using the old noodle."

Pauley said, "Well, sure enough, in about five minutes the jane gets up and goes upstairs. I figure I'll give her about ten minutes alone with him and then I'll make a racket on the door. But she ain't up there over three or four minutes when she comes down. She pushes out of the elevator and crosses the lobby like she was going to a fire. I started to say something to her, but then I figure I ain't got nothing on her and I'm going to have enough trouble with Mallory, anyway. So I decides to let her go, since she ain't a guest in the hotel, and if she'd make a squawk I'd be out on a limb.

"So I go up to Mallory's room, 602, and there's been a fight, plenty of fight. A couple of chairs is busted, a mirror's smashed, and this guy Mallory's lying in the middle of the bed dead to the world from a sock on the bean. The fight must have made something of a racket, but it just happens there's no one below and the people on the sides and across the corridor were out. Well, I make a dive for this guy's pulse and I can feel his pump working. It's faint and stringy, but still a pulse. So I grab the telephone and tell Mamie at the switchboard to get an emergency ambulance. About five minutes later an ambulance shows up and they go to work on this guy."

"Did he regain consciousness?" Mason asked.

"No, he was out like a light," Pauley said. "Well, of course I want to keep the name of the hotel out of it. No one knows anything about the fight, so I persuade the ambulance boys to take him down the freight elevator and out through the alley. Now then, here's the funny part of it: About that time, another ambulance shows up. Mamie says she only put in one call, but records show there were two calls, both of 'em from women with young voices. Now figure that one out. I can't do it, unless that red-headed baby sapped him to sleep, and then went down and ordered a wagon for him."

Mason nodded. Pauley pushed the frayed, wet end of the cigar back into his mouth, and scraped a match into flame. Mason glanced at Paul Drake over the detective's head and raised furtive eyebrows. Drake nodded in answer to the lawyer's unspoken question and said, "I wonder if you'd like to see the way a detective works, Perry. Jim's going up and give the room a once-over and see if he can find out anything that'll be a clue to who did the job. As soon as I saw you drive up, and knowing the way *you* work on a case, I figured you might like to see a real detective in action."

Pauley puffed out several mouthfuls of white smoke from the moist cigar and said deprecatingly, "Aw, I ain't no genius. I just know my business, that's all."

"Sure thing," Mason said, "I'd like to see Pauley in action."

"Well," Pauley said slowly, "of course the police might not like it if I took someone else in. They usually want house detectives to keep in the background while a bunch of hams, who are appointed because they've got political pull somewhere, go in and mess the clues up. But, if you fellows promise not to touch anything, we'll go up and give it a quick once-over. Maybe I can give Mr. Mason a pointer or two, at that." He walked toward the elevator, jabbed a pudgy forefinger against the button, and tilted his head slightly backward so the cigar smoke just missed his right eye. After a moment, the elevator cage appeared. Pauley entered as soon as the door slid open. Mason hesitated long enough to say to Drake in a surreptitious undertone, "Was one of your men on the job, Paul?"

Drake nodded, then followed the house man into the elevator.

"Six," Pauley said. The elevator shot upward and stopped. Pauley said, "This way, boys," and walked down the long corridor. Drake said to Mason in a low voice, "With any luck, one of my men followed her, but don't let Pauley even suspect it."

They followed the house detective to a room near the end of the corridor. He produced a passkey, opened the door, and said, "Be sure not to touch anything."

A chair was overturned, two of the rungs smashed. A floor lamp had been knocked over and the bulb had exploded into myriad fragments of frosty glass which twinkled up from the carpet like bits of ice on a strip of pavement. A mirror, pulled loose from its fastenings, had plummeted downward to the floor and cracked into numerous wedge-shaped segments, some of which were still held in place by the frame of the mirror, while others were littered about the floor. There was a depression in the white counterpane of the bed where a man's body had been stretched out. A Gladstone bag, labeled "WANTED IN CABIN S.S. 'MONTEREY,'" was lying on the floor. Several articles of wearing apparel had been jerked from it. A light wardrobe trunk was standing open. A small portable typewriter was lying bottom-side-up on the floor. The cover of the typewriter case also bore a sticker, "WANTED IN STATEROOM S.S. 'MONTEREY.'" The closet door was partially open, disclosing three or four suits. Mason's eyes focused upon a brief case. A sharp knife had cut around the lock, leaving a flap of leather dangling grotesquely.

"The red-head tried to roll him," Pauley announced, "and he caught her at it. She konked him and then decided to take a look around, probably looking for money."

"Then this red-headed girl must have been a pretty hard customer," Mason said.

Pauley laughed grimly and waved a hand at the wreckage. "Don't that look like it?" he asked. Mason nodded. "One of the first things I've got to do," Pauley remarked, pulling a pencil from his pocket, "is to make an inventory of the stuff that's here. When this man wakes up, he'll claim a lot of stuff is missing, and he's as like as not to to claim some of it was taken *after* he went to the hospital because the hotel didn't use proper diligence in safeguarding the stuff he'd left behind. . . . Oh, you've got to be on to all the tricks to handle the stuff that crops up in a hotel!"

"I'll tell the world," Drake said. "You know, Perry, lots of people think a house detective hasn't got so much on the ball as some of the other boys because he isn't always out on the firing line, but you can take it from me a good house detective has to have everything."

Mason nodded and said, "Well, I have an idea we'd better be going, Paul."

"Thought you were going to stick around," Pauley said.

"No, I just wanted to get a slant on how you went at things," Mason said. "You're going to make a complete inventory now?"

"That's right."

"You don't mean to say you can make an inventory of every little thing that's in the room here."

"Sure I can. And you'll be surprised at how fast I do it."

Mason said, "I'd like to see that inventory when you get done, just to see how you go about it and how you list the stuff."

Pauley pulled a notebook from his pocket and said, "Sure thing."

"We'll drop in after a while," Mason said. "In the meantime, thanks a lot, and it was a real pleasure to see how you worked. A lot of people wouldn't have noticed that girl in the lobby."

Pauley nodded in agreement. "She was clever as hell. Just standing up and giving a little slant to the eyebrows was all the signal she gave. She'd evidently picked him up somewhere and had a date with him here in the hotel."

"Well," Mason said, nudging Drake in the ribs, "let's go."

Pauley saw them as far as the elevator, then returned to finish taking his inventory. Drake said, "Didn't know whether

16

you wanted to play along with him or not, Perry, but I figured I'd give you a chance in case you did. He's a pompous bird, but he really knows the hotel game. A little flattery works wonders with him."

"I just wanted to take a look at the room," Mason said. "The way I figure it, the bishop was tailed to my office and found it out. He wanted to ditch the shadow, so he left his cab driver holding the sack and beat it back here. The boys who were interested in him were relying on the chap who was doing the shadowing to keep the bishop from coming back unexpectedly, so they'd have time to go through the luggage. The bishop came in and surprised them and there was a fight."

"Where does that leave the red-headed dame in the lobby?" Drake asked.

"That's what we've got to find out. I hope your men managed to pick her up."

"I think they did. Charlie Downes was on the job with orders to tail anyone who showed an interest in the bishop. I'll ring up the office and see if he's reported."

Drake called from a telephone booth in the lobby, talked for a few minutes and emerged grinning. "Check," he said. "Charlie telephoned in just a minute ago. He's down on Adams Street, camped in front of an apartment house. The red-headed dame went in there."

"Okay," Mason said, "let's go."

Drake had his own car and he made time through the traffic. Arriving at the Adams Street address, he slowed his car behind an old model Chevrolet which was parked at the curb. A man slid out from behind the wheel and walked slowly toward them. "What d'ya know?" Paul Drake asked.

Charlie Downes, a tall, gangling individual, held a pendulous cigarette from his lower lip. He stood so the two men were looking at his profile. He spoke from the right side of his mouth, which was toward them, while his eyes remained fixed on the apartment house. The cigarette bobbed up and down as he talked.

"This red-headed jane gave the bishop a tumble. He handed her the high-sign and went on up to his room, 602. A little

17

while later the jane went up. I didn't dare to follow her, but I noticed the indicator on the elevator went to six, and then stopped. A couple of minutes later she came down looking plenty excited. She walked across the lobby, went down the street to a drug store, and telephoned. Then she came out, flagged a cab, and came here."

"Make any attempt to break her trail?" Mason asked.

"No."

"Where's she located here?" Mason asked.

"She looked in the lower mail box on the righthand side. I took a look at the name on that box. It's Janice Seaton, and the number's 328. I buzzed a couple of apartments, got a ring and went on in. The elevator was at the third floor. So then I came back and telephoned the office and waited for instructions."

"Good boy," Drake said. "I think you've got something. Stick around here, Charlie, and if she comes out, tag her. We're going up."

The operative nodded and climbed back into his car.

Drake noticed Mason regarding the car and said, "The only kind of a car for a detective to have. Common enough so it doesn't attract attention, dependable enough so it'll go anywhere, and if a man wants to crowd someone into a curb, one more dent in the fenders doesn't mean anything."

Mason grinned and said, "I don't suppose we give this baby a buzz, do we, Paul?"

"Not a chance. We don't give her an opportunity to set the stage. We come down on her like a thousand bricks. Let's buzz a couple of other tenants." He selected a couple of apartments at random and rang the bells until an electric buzzing announced the releasing of the door catch. Pushing open the door, Drake held it for the lawyer, and the two men started climbing the stairs. They found Apartment 328 and listened for a moment in front of the door. Sounds of rapid and purposeful motion reached their ears.

"Packing up," Drake said.

Mason nodded and tapped gently with the tips of his fingers on the panels. A woman's voice on the other side of the door, sounding thin and frightened, said, "Who is it?"

Mason said, "Special delivery."

"Shove it under the door, please."

"There's two cents due on it," Mason remarked.

"Just a moment," the voice said, and steps receded from the door, only to return a moment later as someone made a futile attempt to push two copper pennies through the bottom of the door.

"Go ahead and open the door," Mason said. "I'm a mailman. What the hell do I care!" The lock clicked back. The door opened a crack. Mason pushed the toe of his shoe through the door. The young woman gave a little scream and tried to push it closed. Mason opened the door easily and said, "No need to get excited, Janice. We want to talk with you." He noticed the suitcase on the bed, the trunk, which had been dragged from the closet into the center of the floor, the pile of wearing apparel on the bed and said, "Going places, were you?"

"Who are you and what do you mean by getting in here this way? Where's the special delivery letter?"

Mason indicated a chair and said, "Sit down, Paul, and be comfortable." The detective seated himself, and Mason sat down on the edge of the bed. The girl stared at them from frantic blue eyes. Her hair was the color of spun copper, and she had the smooth complexion which usually goes with such hair. She was slender, well-formed, athletic, and very frightened.

"You might as well sit down, too," Mason told her.

"Who are you? What do you mean by coming in here this way?"

"We want to find out about Bishop Mallory."

"I don't know what you're talking about. I don't know any Bishop Mallory."

"You were over at the Regal Hotel," Mason said.

"I was not!" she blazed, with every evidence of righteous indignation.

"You went up to Mallory's room. The house detective spotted you in the lobby and saw you give the bishop the high-sign when he came in. We may be able to help you, sister, but not unless you come clean."

"You can understand," Drake added, "what a spot *you're* in. As nearly as we can find out, you were the last person to see the bishop alive."

She thrust her clenched fist against her teeth, pressing until the skin around the knuckles grew white. Her eyes were dark with terror. "Alive," she exclaimed. "He's not dead?"

"What do *you* think?" Drake asked.

Abruptly she sat down and started to cry. Mason, his eyes tender with sympathy, glanced across at Paul Drake and shook a warning head. "Not too thick," he said.

Drake remarked impatiently, "If you don't get them on the run, you can't chase them around. Leave it to me." He got to his feet, placed a palm on the girl's forehead, pushed the head back and pulled her handkerchief from her eyes. "Did you kill him?" he asked.

"No!" she cried. "I tell you I don't know him. I don't know what you're talking about, and besides he isn't dead."

Mason said, "Let me handle this for a minute, Paul. Now listen, Janice, it happens that several people were watching Bishop Mallory. I'm not going to tell you who they were nor why they were watching him, but he was shadowed when he entered his hotel. You were seated in the lobby and gave him a high-sign. He motioned for you to wait a little and then come up to his room. You gave him four or five minutes, then went up in the elevator. After a little while you came down, and you were plenty excited. All of that time you were being shadowed by my men, who are trained to remember people. You don't stand any chance whatever of lying out of it. Now, then, after you left the bishop's place you went to a telephone and telephoned for an ambulance to come and pick up the bishop. That put you in a spot. I'm trying to give you a chance to get out."

"Who are you?" she asked.

"A friend of Bishop Mallory's."

"How do I know that?"

"Just at present," he said, "you take my word for it."

"I'd want something more than that."

"Okay, then, I'm a friend of yours."

"How do I know that?"

"Because I'm sitting here talking with you instead of telephoning police headquarters."

"He isn't dead?" she asked.

"No," Mason said, "he isn't dead."

Drake frowned impatiently and said, "You'll never get anywhere this way, Perry. She's going to lie now."

The girl whirled to the tall detective and said, "You shut up! He'll get a lot farther with me than you would."

Drake said impersonally, "I know the type, Perry. You've got to keep them on the run. Get them frightened and keep them that way. Try to play square with them and they'll slip out from under."

She ignored the comment, turned to Perry Mason and said, "I'll play square with you. I answered an ad in a paper."

"And met the bishop that way?"

"Yes."

"What was the ad?"

She hesitated a moment, then tilted her chin and said, "He advertised for a trained nurse who was dependable and trustworthy."

"You're a trained nurse?"

"Yes."

"How many other people answered the ad?"

"I don't know."

"When did *you* answer it?"

"Yesterday."

"Did the bishop give his name and address?"

"No, only a blind box."

"So you answered the ad. Then what happened?"

"Then the bishop telephoned me and said he liked my letter and wanted a personal interview."

"When was that?"

"Late last night."

"So you went to the hotel this morning for that interview?"

"No, I went to the hotel last night, and he hired me."

"Did he say what for?"

"He said he wanted me to nurse a patient."

"You're a registered nurse?" Paul Drake interrupted.

"Yes."

21

"Show me," Drake said.

She opened the suitcase, took out a manila envelope, handed it to the detective and immediately turned her eyes back to Mason. She was more sure of herself now, more calmly competent, more wary, and more watchful.

"So Bishop Mallory hired you?" Mason asked.

For a moment her eyes wavered. Then she shook her head and said, "No."

"What paper was it in?"

"I can't remember. It was in one of the evening papers a day or two ago. Someone called the ad to my attention."

"So Bishop Mallory hired you?" Mason asked.

"Yes."

"Did he say what was wrong with the patient?"

"No, he didn't. I gathered that it was a case of insanity in the family or something of that sort."

"Why all the packing up?" Paul Drake asked, handing back the manila envelope.

"Because Bishop Mallory told me I'd have to go with him and the patient on a trip."

"Did he say where?"

"No."

"And he told you to meet him in the hotel?"

"Yes. And I wasn't to talk with him in the lobby. He was to nod if everything was all right, and I was to go up to his room after five minutes."

"Why all the mystery?" Drake asked.

"I don't know. He didn't tell me, and I didn't ask him. He was a bishop, so I knew he was all right, and he was paying good wages. Also, you know how some mental cases are. They go wild if they think they're under treatment or even observation."

"So you went up to the room," Mason said. "What did you find?"

"I found things all topsy-turvy. The bishop was lying on the floor. He had a concussion. His pulse was weak but steady. I picked him up and got him to bed. It was a job—an awful job."

"Did you see anyone in the room?"

"No."

"Was the door locked or unlocked?"

"It was open an inch or two."

"Did you see anyone in the corridor?" Mason asked.

"You mean when I went up to see the bishop?"

"Yes."

"No."

"Did you see anyone coming down in the elevator just as you went up?"

"No."

"Why didn't you notify the hotel authorities when you found the bishop?"

"I didn't think there was any need. They couldn't have done anything. I went out and telephoned for an ambulance."

"And then came here and got ready to skip out?" Drake asked sneeringly.

"I wasn't getting ready to skip out. I'd done this earlier in the day because the bishop said I'd have to travel. He said the patient was sailing on the *Monterey.*"

"What're your plans now?"

"I'm just going to wait here until I hear from the bishop. I don't think he's seriously hurt. He'll be conscious in an hour or two at the latest unless there are sclerotic conditions."

Mason got to his feet and said, "Okay, Paul, I think she's told us everything she knows. Let's go."

Drake said, "You're going to let her get away with this, Perry?"

The lawyer's eyes were stern. "Of course I am. The trouble with you, Paul, is that you deal so much with crooks you don't know how to treat a woman who's on the square."

Drake sighed and said, "You win. Let's go."

Janice Seaton came close to Perry Mason, placed her hand on his arm and gave it a friendly squeeze. "Thank you *so* much," she said, "for being a gentleman."

They stepped into the corridor, heard the door slam behind them. A moment later there was a click as the key turned in the lock. Drake said to Mason, "What's the idea in being such a softy, Perry? We might have found out something if we'd made her think it was a murder pinch."

"We're finding out plenty the way it is," Mason told him. "That girl's up to something. Make her suspicious and we'll never find out what it is. Let her think she's pulled the wool over our eyes and she'll give us a lead. Put a couple of men on the job. Run over to the Regal Hotel. Hand your friend the house dick a little more salve, and see if you can get a description of some man who came down the stairs to the lobby shortly after the girl went up on the elevator and before the house dick started after her."

"Anything else?" Drake asked.

"Follow the girl wherever she goes, and get that other dope for me just as quickly as you can—you know, the manslaughter business, a line on the bishop and all that. And remember to keep a tail on that bishop. Find out what hospital he's at and get a line on his condition."

"Bet you *four* to one he's a phoney," Drake said.

Mason grinned and said, "No takers—not yet. Call me at the office and keep me posted on developments."

Chapter 3

The five o'clock exodus of workers was swarming down the elevators into the vortex of swirling humanity which flowed along the concrete canyons of the city thoroughfares. Through the windows came the sound of police whistles directing traffic, the clang of signals, the impatient gongs of street cars, the raucous horns of stalled traffic, and the ever present throbbing undertone of sound which comes from idling motors.

Della Street, seated at her secretarial desk, making entries in a ledger, looked up at the grinning figure of Perry Mason as he entered the office. "Well," she asked, "did you have your meeting with Bishop Mallory and find out what it's all about?"

He shook his head and said, "No. The bishop isn't in any condition to keep appointments. He's temporarily indisposed, and probably will be for some time. Get all of the newspapers, Della, both today's and yesterday's. We have a job checking want ads."

She started for the door to the law library, then stopped and said, "Can you tell me what happened, Chief?"

He nodded. "We traced the bishop to his hotel. Someone had tapped him to sleep with a blackjack. We ran onto a red-headed spitfire who strung us along with a lot of fairy stories. But, every once in a while her face slipped and she told the truth, because she couldn't think up the lies fast enough."

"What do we look for in the newspapers?" she asked.

"The red-head said she got in touch with the bishop by answering an ad. She *may* have been telling the truth, because the bishop is probably a stranger in the city. At any rate, we're going to run that angle down and see what we can find. Look under the 'Help Wanted' ads and see if we can find where someone has advertised for a nurse, young, unencumbered,G

25

and willing to travel. . . . Her name, by the way, is Janice Seaton."

"But why would Bishop Mallory want a nurse?" she asked.

"He wants one now," Mason said, grinning, "and perhaps he had some idea of what was coming and wanted to be prepared. He *told* her she was to travel with a patient."

Della Street, moving with the crisp efficiency of a thoroughly competent secretary, slipped through the door into the library, to return in a few moments with an armful of newspapers. Mason cleared a space on his desk, selected a cigarette and said, "Okay, let's start."

Together, they read through the want ads in the newspapers. At the end of fifteen minutes, Mason looked up, blinked his eyes and said, "Find anything, Della?"

She shook her head, finished the last column of ads and said, "Nothing doing, Chief."

Mason twisted his face into an exaggerated grimace and said, "Think of how Paul Drake's going to rub it into me. I figured we could get farther by giving her plenty of rope, and I was foolish enough to think I could tell when she was lying and when she was telling us the truth."

"You figured she was telling the truth about the ad?"

"I thought so, yes. Perhaps not the whole truth, but enough of it to give us a line on what was happening."

"What gave you that idea?" she asked.

"Well," Mason said slowly, "you know how it is when people lie at high speed without having any chance to make things up beforehand. They'll try to follow the truth as far as possible and then figure some falsehood which will link one batch of truth with another batch of truth. There's a certain tempo that gets in their voices when they're running along over ground they're certain of, and then they slow down a bit when they're thinking up the connecting links. I figured this ad business was on the square."

Mason got to his feet and started pacing the office floor, his thumbs hooked in the armholes of his vest, his head tilted slightly forward. "The hell of it is," he said, "Paul Drake wanted to get rough. He figured we could get somewhere getting her frightened. He might have been right. But you know how red-heads are. And this one looked able to take care of herself. I figured she'd flare up and start fighting until she got hysterical. I felt certain we'd stand more chance giving her plenty of rope and being kind to her than we would by going after her, hammer and tongs."

The telephone rang. Della Street, with her eyes still on one of the newspapers, groped for the receiver, found it and said, "Perry Mason's office," then extended the receiver toward the lawyer. "Paul Drake on the line," she said.

Mason picked up the receiver and said, "Hello, Paul. What's new?"

Drake's drawling voice showed a trace of excitement. "I've got the dope on that manslaughter for you, Perry," he said. "At least I'm hoping it's the right dope. A woman and a man had been down to Santa Ana getting married. They were on their way back to Los Angeles. The woman was driving. She'd had a few drinks. She ran into a car driven by an old rancher, a chap who was in the late seventies. Now, here's the funny thing about it: Nothing much was done at the time. They took the woman's name and address. The man died a couple of days later. But it wasn't until four months after that a warrant was filed for the arrest of the woman on a manslaughter charge. That looks sort of fishy on the face of it."

"Who was the woman?"

"She had been Julia Branner," Drake said, "but at the moment she was Mrs. Oscar Brownley. And in case you don't know it, Oscar Brownley was the son of Renwold C. Brownley."

Mason gave a low whistle and said, "Wasn't there some sort of scandal about that marriage, Paul?"

"Remember," Drake said, "that was back in 1914. Brownley made nearly all of his money on the big bull market and was wise enough to get out and duck out just before the crash in '29. Brownley in 1914 was dabbling around in real estate. Twelve years later he was a millionaire."

"Couldn't they have arrested the woman easily enough if they'd really wanted her?" Mason asked.

"No. She and Oscar had a fight with the old man and went places. About a year later, Oscar came back. The old man had turned some good real estate deals in the meantime. He rode the crest of the subdivision wave, then switched into the stock market, made a killing, and got out."

"Where's Oscar now? Didn't he die?"

"That's right. He died two or three years ago."

"He left a daughter, didn't he?"

"Yes. There's something more or less mysterious about that daughter. You know, Renwold was all wrapped up in Oscar. It wasn't until after Oscar died that he was willing to recognize the granddaughter. You see, he'd bitterly disapproved of the marriage, and apparently figured the daughter was a mistake on the part of the mother, rather than any offspring of his son. Two years ago he hunted up the granddaughter and took her in to live with him. No great commotion was made over it. The girl simply moved in with Renwold."

Mason frowned thoughtfully, clamped the receiver to his ear with his left hand, made drumming motions with the fingertips of his right hand on the edge of the desk. "Then the mother of the girl who is now living in the lap of luxury in Renwold Brownley's Beverly Hills residence is a fugitive from justice on a manslaughter warrant issued in Orange County twenty-two years ago?"

"That's right," Drake said.

"This thing," Mason told him, "commences to be *really* interesting. What do you hear from the bishop, Paul?"

"Still unconscious at the Receiving Hospital, but surgeons say it's nothing serious. He'll regain consciousness any minute. They're taking him to a private hospital. I'll find out where it is and let you know."

"You're keeping shadows on that Seaton girl?"

"I'll tell the world. I've got two men there, one watching the front of the apartment house and one the back. I wish you had let me tear into her, Perry. We had her on the run and then . . ."

Mason chuckled and said, "You don't know your red-heads, Paul. It'll turn out all right. Find out all you can about that Brownley angle and let me know just as soon as you get anything definite."

"By the way," Drake said, "I found out a little more about

the bishop. He came in six days ago on the *Monterey* and was in the Palace Hotel in San Francisco for four days. Then he came down here."

"Well, see what you can find out in San Francisco," Mason said. "Find out who called on him at the hotel and all that sort of stuff. Let me know as soon as you get anything else. I'll be here for an hour or so. Then Della and I are going out to get some eats."

Mason hung up the receiver and resumed his pacing of the office. He had taken only two turns, however, when Della Street said excitedly, "Wait a minute, Chief. You were right, after all. Here it is!"

"What?"

"The ad."

He strode to her secretarial desk, stood with one hand on her shoulder, leaning over, looking at the ad she was indicating with the point of a polished nail: "IF THE DAUGHTER OF CHARLES W. AND GRACE SEATON, WHO FORMERLY LIVED IN RENO, NEVADA, WILL GET IN TOUCH WITH BOX XYZ LOS ANGELES 'EXAMINER' SHE WILL LEARN SOMETHING OF GREAT ADVANTAGE TO HERSELF."

Mason whistled and said, "In the personal column, eh?"

Della Street nodded, grinned up at him and said, "You see, I have more faith in your judgment than you have. If you thought she was telling the truth about an ad, I was willing to gamble on it. But when we couldn't find it in the 'Help Wanted' or 'Business Opportunities,' I decided to take a look at the 'Personals.'"

Mason said, "Let's look at the *Times* and see if he has one in there. When was this?"

"Yesterday," she said.

Mason pulled out the *Times* classified ad section of the same date, ran hurriedly down the "Personals" and then gave a low whistle and said, "Look at this, Della."

Together, they stared at an ad reading: "WANTED: INFORMATION WHICH WILL ENABLE ME TO GET IN TOUCH WITH A JANICE SEATON WHO WILL BE TWENTY-TWO YEARS OF AGE ON FEBRUARY 19TH. SHE IS A GRADUATE NURSE, RED-HEADED, BLUE EYES, ATTRACTIVE, WEIGHT ABOUT A HUNDRED AND

FIFTEEN, HEIGHT FIVE FEET ONE. IS THE DAUGHTER OF CHARLES W. SEATON WHO WAS KILLED SIX MONTHS AGO IN AN AUTOMOBILE ACCIDENT. $25 REWARD TO THE FIRST PERSON FURNISHING AUTHENTIC INFORMATION. BOX ABC LOS ANGELES 'TIMES.' "

Della Street picked up a pair of scissors and snipped both ads from the papers. "Well?" she asked.

Mason grinned and said, "Saves my face with Paul Drake."

"And," she told him, "I take it the plot thickens?"

Mason frowned and said, "Yes, it thickens like the gravy I made on my last camping trip—all in a bunch of lumps, which don't seem to be smoothing out."

She laughed up at him and said, "Did you apologize for the gravy, Chief?"

"Hell, no!" he told her. "I told the boys that it was the latest thing out, something I'd learned from the chef in a famous New York restaurant; that it was Thousand-Island Gravy.

"Ring up Paul Drake, tell him we're going to dinner. Don't tell him anything about the ad. Let's see if he finds it. Tell him to meet us here after dinner."

"Listen, Chief," she told him, "aren't you sort of getting the cart before the horse? We're finding out a lot *about* the bishop, but not very much *for* him. After all, what the bishop wanted to know was about a manslaughter case."

Mason nodded thoughtfully and said, "That's what he *said* he wanted to know about. But I smelled something big in the wind, and the scent keeps getting stronger. The thing which bothers me is that it's getting too strong. I tried putting two and two together, and the answer I get is six."

Chapter 4

Perry Mason was in a rare good humor as he ordered cocktails and dinner. Della Street, watching him with the insight which comes from years of close association, said, as she tilted her cocktail glass, "Riding the crest, aren't you, Chief?"

He nodded, eyes brimming with the joy of living. "How I love a mystery, Della," he said. "I hate routine. I hate details. I like the thrill of matching my wits with crooks. I like to have people lie to me and catch them in their lies. I love to listen to people talk and wonder how much of it is true and how much of it is false. I want life, action, shifting conditions. I like to fit facts together, bit by bit, like the pieces of a jigsaw puzzle."

"And you think this stuttering bishop is trying to slip something over on you?" she asked.

Mason twisted the stem of his empty cocktail glass in his fingers. "Darned if I know, Della," he told her. "The bishop's playing a deep game. I sensed it the minute he came into the office, and somehow, I have the feeling that he wanted to keep me in the dark as to his real purpose. That's why I'm going to get such a kick out of outguessing him, figuring what he wants before he's willing to let me know just *what* he wants. Come on, let's dance." He swept her out on the dance floor, where they moved with the perfect rhythm of long practice together. The dance over, they returned to find the first course of the dinner set before them.

"Tell me about it," she invited him, "if you want to."

"I want to," Mason said. "I want to run over all of the facts, just to see if I can't fit them together. Some of them you know, some of them you don't know.

"Let's begin at the beginning. A man who claims to be an Australian bishop comes to call on me. He's excited and he

31

stutters. Every time he stutters, he gets mad at himself. Now why?"

"Because," she said, "he knows that a bishop shouldn't stutter. Perhaps it's some habit he's developed recently, due to an emotional shock, and he's wondering what will happen if he returns to Australia and stutters."

"Swell," he told her. "That's a good logical explanation. That's the one which occurred to me right at the start. But suppose the man isn't a bishop but is some crook masquerading, for one reason or another, as Bishop Mallory of Sydney, Australia. He's inclined to stutter when he becomes excited. Therefore, he tries his darnedest *not* to stutter, the result being that he stutters just that much more. He's afraid that stuttering is going to give him away." She nodded slowly.

"Now then," Mason said, "this bishop wants to see me about a manslaughter case. He doesn't mention names, but it's virtually certain the manslaughter case is one involving the Julia Branner who became Mrs. Oscar Brownley, Oscar Brownley being the older of Renwold C. Brownley's two sons.

"I don't need to tell you about Brownley. The younger son died six or seven years ago. Oscar went away with his wife, no one knows just where. Then he came back. The woman didn't. Manslaughter charges were pending against her in Orange County. But those charges weren't filed until some time after the automobile accident."

"Well?" she asked.

"Well," Mason said, "suppose I should tell you that Renwold Brownley knew that his son Oscar was coming back to him and was afraid the woman was going to *try* to come back. Wouldn't it be a smart move for Renwold Brownley to pull some political wires and get a warrant of arrest issued for her? Then the minute she returned to California he could have her thrown into jail on a manslaughter charge."

Della Street nodded absently, pushed back her soup dish and said, "Aren't there two grandchildren living with Brownley?"

"That's right," he said. "Philip Brownley, whose father was the younger son, and a girl whose first name I've forgotten, who's the daughter of Oscar. Now Bishop Mallory comes over on the *Monterey*, stays four or five days in San Francisco, puts some ads in the local papers and . . ."

"Wait a minute," she interrupted. "I've just remembered something. You say the bishop came over on the *Monterey*?"

"Yes, why?"

She laughed nervously and said, "Chief, you know a lot about human nature. Why do stenographers, secretaries and shop girls read the society news?"

"I'll bite. Why do they?"

She shrugged her shoulders. For a moment her eyes were wistful. "I'm darned if I know, Chief. I wouldn't want to live unless I could work for a living, and yet I like to read about who's at Palm Springs, who's doing what in Hollywood and all the rest of it, and every secretary I know does the same thing."

Watching her narrowly, Mason said, "Skip the preliminaries, Della, and tell me what it's all about."

She said slowly, "I happen to remember that Janice Alma Brownley, the granddaughter of Renwold C. Brownley, was a passenger on the *Monterey* from Sydney to San Francisco, and the newspapers said that the attractive young heiress was the center of social life aboard the ship, or words to that effect, if you get what I mean. You see, Chief, *you* don't know the granddaughter's first name, but I can tell you lots about her."

Mason stared across the table at her and said, "Twelve."

"What?" she asked.

"Twelve," he repeated, a twinkle in his eyes.

"Chief, what on earth are you talking about?"

"I told you a minute ago that when I added two and two in this case I didn't get four, but six, and it bothered me," he said. "Now I add two and two and make twelve."

"Twelve what?"

He shook his head and said, "Let's not even *think* of it for a while. It's not often that we have a chance to relax, Della. Let's eat, drink and be merry, have a few dances, go back to the office and get Paul Drake in for a conference. By that time the thing I'm chasing will probably turn out to be just a mirage. But in the meantime," he said, somewhat wistfully, "just in

33

case it shouldn't be a mirage, what a gosh-awful case it would be. A regular humdinger of a case. A gee whillikins of a case!"

"Tell me, Chief."

He shook his head and said, "It can't be true, Della. It's just a mirage. Let's not talk about it and then we won't be disappointed if Paul Drake unearths information which shows we're all wet."

She regarded him thoughtfully and said, "Do you mean that this girl . . ."

"Tut, tut," he told her warningly, "don't argue with the boss. Come on, Della, this is a fox-trot. Remember now, we're giving our minds a recess."

Mason refused to be hurried through the dinner, or to discuss any business. Della Street matched his mood. For more than an hour they enjoyed one of those rare periods of intimacy which comes to people who have worked together, sharing disappointments and triumphs, who understand each other so perfectly that there is no need for any of the little hypocrisies which are so frequently the rule rather than the exception in human contacts.

Not until after the dessert had been taken away and the lawyer had sipped the very last drop of his *liqueur* did he sigh and say, "Well, Della, let's go back to our mirage-chasing and prove that it really is a mirage after all."

"You think it is?" she asked.

"I don't know," he told her, "but I'm afraid to think it isn't. In any event, let's telephone Drake to meet us at the office."

"Listen, Chief," she said, "I've been thinking. Suppose this woman, knowing there was a felony warrant out for her arrest in California, fled to Australia and suppose . . ."

"Not a word," he said, gripping her shoulder. "Let's not go jumping around in the clouds. We'll keep our feet on the ground. You telephone Paul Drake to meet us at the office, and I'll get a cab."

She nodded, but her eyes were preoccupied. "Of course," she said, "if he shouldn't be the real bishop but should be an impostor . . ."

Mason pointed a rigid forefinger at her, crooked his thumb as though it had been the trigger of a revolver, and said, "Halt, or I fire."

She laughed and said, "I'll call Paul while I'm powdering my nose, Chief," and vanished into the dressing room.

Paul Drake tapped on the door of Perry Mason's private office and Della Street let him in. "You two look well fed," Drake remarked, grinning at them.

Mason had lost the carefree mannerism of the cabaret. His face was thoughtful, his eyes half closed in concentration. "What about the bishop, Paul?" he asked.

"The bishop is at present perfectly able to navigate under his own power," Drake said. "He's out of the hospital and back at his hotel. He can't wear a hat, though. His head is so covered with bandages that only one eye and the tip of his nose are showing. According to last reports, he's pursuing the even tenor of his ecclesiastical ways."

"And how about the Seaton girl?"

"Still in her apartment on West Adams Street. She hasn't budged. Apparently she's waiting for a call from the bishop and isn't going to leave until it comes in."

Mason frowned thoughtfully and said, "That doesn't make sense, Paul."

"It's one of the few things that does make sense," the detective rejoined. "She was packing up when we busted in on her. Evidently she was getting ready to go places. She admitted she was to travel with the bishop or with some patient he was to get for her. So she's waiting for the bishop to give her definite instructions. She hasn't stuck her nose outdoors since the bishop went to the hospital."

"Hasn't been out to dinner?"

"Hasn't even opened the back door to dump out any garbage," Drake said.

"You've got two men watching the front and back of the apartment?"

"That's right. The man who followed her to the apartment was watching the front, and I had an operative at the back within five minutes of the time we left there."

Mason said, "Della supplied a fact which may be important. Janice Alma Brownley came over on the *Monterey* from Australia."

"Well," Drake asked, "what about it?"

"Bishop Mallory came over on the same ship. They were together for two or three weeks on shipboard. And, mind you, unless there's a nigger in the woodpile somewhere, the woman the bishop is inquiring about on the manslaughter business is the mother of the Brownley girl."

Drake frowned thoughtfully.

Mason said, "Della and I have been toying around with an idea, Paul. It may be goofy. I haven't dared to think about it out loud. I want you to listen to it and see what *you* think."

"Go to it," Drake told him. "I'm always willing to punch holes in ideas."

"Suppose," Mason said, "the Branner woman skipped out to Australia. Suppose, after Oscar Brownley went back to the States, she had a baby. Suppose Bishop Mallory, being at that time a Church of England minister, was given the child to put in a good home somewhere. Suppose he gave her to a family named Seaton, and then suppose when he came to the United States on the *Monterey* he found some girl on the ship posing as Janice Brownley and *knew* she was an impostor; but suppose he wanted to play his cards pretty close to his chest and get some definite proof before he started any fireworks, and among other things, wanted to dig up the real Brownley girl—now why wouldn't that fit with the facts?"

Drake thought for a moment and then said, "No, Perry, that's goofy. In the first place, it's all surmise. In the second place, the girl couldn't have been received into the Brownley household without the mother knowing about it, and if it *had* been the wrong girl she'd have raised merry hell."

"Suppose," Mason interrupted, "the mother was out of the state and *didn't* know about it but is just finding it out. Then she'd come on here to really raise some hell."

"Well," Drake said, "she hasn't showed up. That's the best answer to that. Also, don't forget that good-looking gals change a lot from the time they're little pink morsels of humanity until they blossom forth into dazzling heiresses. Bishop Mallory is probably far more interested in ecclesiastical duties than tagging babies whom he has farmed out for adoption. . . . No, Perry, I think you've got a wrong hunch. But *this* may be the case: Someone may be going to pull a shake-down and in order to work it they need *a* Bishop Mallory to lay the foundation, so if they had a fake Bishop Mallory call on a credulous but aggressive lawyer and spill a sob-sister story they might throw enough monkey wrenches in the Brownley machinery to get a rake-off."

"So you think the bishop is a fake?" Mason asked.

"Right from the first," Drake said, "I figured this bishop was a crook. I don't like that stuttering business, Perry."

Mason said slowly, "Neither do I, when you come right down to it."

"Well," Drake said, grinning, "we're right down to it."

"So," Mason said, "I think we'll talk with Bishop Mallory again—that is, unless he gets in touch with me first. How long's he been at the hotel, Paul?"

"Around half an hour I'd say. They patched him up at the hospital, and after he recovered consciousness he was none the worse for wear, except for the headache and the flock of bandages on his head."

"What did he tell the police?"

"He said he opened the door of his room and someone jumped out from behind the door and hit him, and that's all he remembers."

Mason frowned and said, "That wouldn't account for the broken mirror and the busted chair, Paul. There was a fight in that room."

Drake shrugged his shoulders and said, "All I know is that that's the story he told the police. Of course, Perry, sometimes when a man's been given a knock on the bean that way he forgets a good deal of what happened."

"You've got a man trailing the bishop?" Mason asked.

"Two men," Drake said. "Two men in two separate cars. We're not letting him out of our sight."

Mason said thoughtfully, "Let's go talk with this Seaton girl again, and let's take Della along. The kid's a red-headed spitfire, but she may loosen up if Della talks to her."

Drake's voice showed resentment. "We'll never get anything out of her *now*," he said.

"Why the accent on the now?" Mason asked.

"I don't like the way you handled it, Perry. I know her type. We should have kept her on the run, made her think the bishop had been murdered, pretended she was a logical suspect, and then she'd have told the truth in order to clear her skirts."

"She told some of the truth, anyway," Mason said, "about getting in touch with him through an ad, for instance." Mason motioned to Della Street, who handed over the ads she had clipped from the personal columns. Mason gave them to the detective who stared at them frowningly and said, "What the devil's the idea, Perry?"

"I don't know, Paul, unless it's the way I outlined to you. Have you heard anything more from Australia, Paul?"

"No. I've wired my correspondents for a description and asked them to cable the bishop's present address."

Mason said thoughtfully, "I keep thinking that Seaton girl holds the key to this thing. We'll drop in on her, ask a few more questions, and then go see His Nibs, the Stuttering Bishop. And by that time I think we'll have an earful."

Paul Drake said, "Of course, Perry, it's none of *my* business, but why go to all this trouble over a case which probably isn't going to amount to anything, which hasn't paid you any fee, and where no one seems to be in particularly urgent need of your services?"

He shrugged and said, "I'm afraid, Paul, you overlook the potential possibilities of the situation. In the first place, it's a mystery, and you know how I feel about mysteries. In the second place, unless all signs fail, what we're having so far is what is technically known as the 'build-up.'"

"Build-up to what?" Drake asked in his slow drawl.

Mason looked at his wristwatch and said, "My guess is that within twelve hours I'll receive a call from a woman who gives her name either as Julia Branner or Mrs. Oscar Brownley."

The detective said, "You may, at that, Perry. And *she* may be phoney. If she isn't . . . well, you might have *lots* of action."

Mason put on his hat and said, "Come on. Let's go."

They went in Drake's car to the apartment house on West Adams. Behind the windshield of a battered car, a little spot of light marked the glowing end of a cigarette. A figure detached itself from the black shadows and proved to be that of Charlie Downes. "All clear?" Drake asked.

"Everything's under control," the man grinned. "How long do I stay here?"

"You'll be relieved at midnight," Drake said. "Until then, stick on the job. We're going up. She may go out as soon as we leave. If she does, we want to know where she goes."

They took the elevator to the third floor. Drake led the way to Apartment 328 and tapped gently on the panels. There was no answer. He knocked more loudly.

Mason whispered, "Wait a minute, Paul. I've got an idea." He said to Della Street, "Call out, 'Open the door, Janice, this is I.'"

Della Street nodded, placed her mouth close to the door and said, "Open up, Janice. It's I."

Again there was no sound of motion. Mason dropped to his knees, took a long envelope from his pocket, inserted it under the door, moved it back and forth and said, "There's no light in there, Paul."

"The devil!" Paul Drake said.

They stood in a silent, compact group for a moment. Then Drake said, "I'm going down and make certain the back end of the place is covered, and has been covered ever since we left."

"We'll wait here," Mason told him. Drake didn't wait to use the elevator, but ran down the stairs.

"Suppose," Della Street ventured, "that she really couldn't have left the building."

"Well?" Mason asked.

"Then she's in there."

"What do you mean?"

"Perhaps she's . . . you know."

"You mean committed suicide?"

"Yes."

Mason said, "She didn't look like that kind to me, Della. She looked like a fighter. But of course there's *some* chance she's wise enough to have gone into some friend's apartment here in the same building. That's one thing we may have to figure on. Or, she may be inside, playing possum."

They stood in uncomfortable silence, waiting.

Drake came back, panting from his exertion in taking the stairs two at a time, and said, "She's sewed up in the place.

It's a cinch she hasn't left by either the front or the rear. She's bound to be inside. You know, Perry, there's just a chance . . ."

His voice trailed away into silence and Perry said, "Yes, Della was wondering about that. But, somehow, I can't figure her for that sort of a play."

Drake grinned and said, "I know a way we can find out."

"Speaking as a lawyer," Mason observed, "I'd say such a method would be highly illegal."

Drake produced a folding leather tool kit from his pocket and took out some skeleton keys.

"Which'll it be," he asked, "conscience or curiosity?"

Mason said, "Curiosity."

Drake fitted a key in the lock and Mason said to Della, "You'd better keep out of this, Della. Stand in the corridor and don't come in. Then you won't be guilty of anything in case there's a squawk."

Drake clicked back the lock and said, "If you see anybody coming, Della, start knocking on the door. We'll lock it from the inside. When we hear you knock that'll be our signal to keep quiet."

"Suppose it should be the girl herself?" Della Street asked.

"It won't be. She can't have left. But if it *should* be, she's about twenty-one or twenty-two, with dark copper hair that's alive, eyes that have plenty of fire, and a peaches-and-cream complexion. She's easy on the eyes. Try and think up some stall which will take her away and give us a chance to get out. Tell her there's someone waiting in the car downstairs who is very anxious to see her. Don't mention any names, but let her think it's the bishop, and see what her reaction is to that."

"Okay," Della said, "don't worry. I'll work out something."

"She's dynamite," Mason warned. "Don't start an argument with her because I wouldn't put it past her to start hair-pulling."

"Do we switch on the lights?" Drake asked.

"Sure," Mason said.

"Okay, here goes."

"Close the door first," Mason warned.

They closed the door. Drake groped for the light switch and clicked the room into brilliance. Apparently it was exactly as they had seen it earlier in the day. The clothes were piled on the bed, the wardrobe trunk was open in the center of the floor and partially packed.

Mason said in a low voice, "If she did anything, Paul, she did it right after we were here talking with her. You take a look in the bathroom; I'll take the kitchenette."

"Don't forget the big closet behind the bed, either," Drake said. "My God, Perry, I'm afraid to take a look. If we find her dead, it's going to put us in one hell of a spot."

"Are *you*," asked Perry Mason, "telling *me*?"

They separated, made a hasty search of the apartment, and met once more by the bed, with sheepish grins.

"Well, Perry," Drake said, "she out-smarted us. Of course, there's a chance she has a friend here in the building and has gone in with her."

Mason shook his head and said, "If she'd been doing that, she'd probably have finished her packing so she'd be all ready to come back, grab her stuff and make a dash for it just as soon as the coast was clear. No, Paul, she walked out on us through the back door within five minutes of the time we left the place, and before your second man had time to get on the job."

Drake sighed and said, "I guess you're right, Perry. But it makes me sore to think she took me as easily as that. Here I've been sewing the place up tight while she's been on the loose."

Mason said grimly, "Well, we'll go and see the bishop. Della, you go back to the office and stick around. Keep the light on and the outer door open." As he saw the look of inquiry on her face, he said, "I want you to wait for Julia Branner, or Mrs. Oscar Brownley, whatever name she's going under. We'll drive you over to the boulevard and you can get a taxi. Then we'll go on to the Regal Hotel."

Drake left orders his men were to keep a watch of the apartment and report as soon as Janice Seaton returned. They they drove Della Street to the boulevard, saw her headed for the office in a cab, and drove directly to the Regal Hotel. In the hotel, Drake looked around in the lobby and said, "I don't see either of the boys here."

"What does that mean?" Mason asked.

"Probably that he's gone out."

"Meeting the Seaton girl somewhere," Mason surmised.

"I'll hunt up Jim Pauley and see if he knows anything," Drake said. "There he is now, over . . . Hey, Jim!"

The house detective, looking ponderously incongruous in a tuxedo, ducked his bald head in a grinning greeting and came strutting across the lobby. "This Mallory is a Church of England bishop," he said, "and right now he's nursing a mighty sore head. But he's a good sport. He says there is nothing missing and he isn't going to make a squawk about it, so we can hush it up. Under the circumstances, we're ready to meet him halfway. By the way, he went out a while ago and left a letter for Mr. Mason."

Mason and Drake exchanged glances. "A letter for me?" Mason asked.

"Yeah. It's at the desk. I'll get it."

"Take any baggage with him?" Drake asked.

"No. He was just going out for dinner, I think."

The detective stepped behind the counter and took a sealed envelope from a pigeon-hole. The envelope was addressed: "Perry Mason, Attorney at Law. To be delivered to Mr. Mason when he calls this evening."

Mason slit open the envelope. A five-dollar bill was clipped to a sheet of hotel stationery. A brief note read:

"DEAR MR. MASON: *I realized I was being followed shortly after I left your office, so I got the janitor to let me out through the basement and alley. I subsequently telephoned to try and locate my cab, and found that you had paid it off. I am, therefore, reimbursing you herewith.*

Insofar as the advice which you have given me is concerned, I beg you to consider it as bread cast upon the waters, and believe I can assure you that it will be returned a thousandfold.
WILLIAM MALLORY

Mason sighed, pulled the five-dollar bill from the clip, folded it, and slipped it in his vest pocket. "The bishop didn't say when he'd be back, did he?" Mason asked.

Jim Pauley shook his head, said, "A mighty nice chap, the bishop. Didn't seem to resent things at all. He got a lulu of a crack on his head. Couldn't even wear his hat. Had to be all bandaged up like a turban."

Mason nodded to Drake and said significantly, "Suppose you call your office, Paul."

Drake went into the telephone booth and talked for several moments into the transmitter. Then he opened the door of the booth and beckoned to Mason. "My operatives have reported back," he said in a low monotone, keeping his head back in the shadows of the booth. "They followed the bishop to Piers 157-158, Los Angeles harbor. He stopped at a pawnshop on the way, and bought two suitcases and some clothes. They followed him from there to the pier. He went up the gangplank of the S.S. *Monterey*, and he didn't come down again. The *Monterey* sailed tonight for Australia via Honolulu and Pago Pago. My men followed the ship in a speed launch well beyond the breakwater, to make sure the bishop didn't get off. Looks like your friend has taken a run-out powder. Watch your step, Perry. He's a phoney."

Mason shrugged and said, "Let me at that phone, Paul."

Della Street's voice on the line was excited, "Hello, Chief," she said. "You win."

"On what?" he asked.

"Julia Branner is here at the office, waiting for you; says she must see you at once."

Chapter 5

Julia Branner stared at Perry Mason with reddish-brown eyes which matched the glint in her hair. Her face was that of a young woman in the late twenties, save for a line beneath her chin and incipient calipers which stretched from her nose to the corners of her lips when she smiled.

"It's rather unusual for me to see clients at this hour," Mason said.

"I just got in," she told him. "I saw a light in your office, so I came in. Your secretary said you *might* see me."

"Live here in the city?" Mason asked.

"I'm staying with a friend at 214-A West Beechwood. I'm going to share an apartment with her."

"Married or single?" Mason asked casually.

"I go by the name of Miss Branner."

"You're working?"

"Not at present, but I've been working until recently. I have a little money."

"You've been working here in this city?"

"No, not here."

"Where?"

"Does that make any difference?"

"Yes," Mason told her.

"In Salt Lake City."

"And you say you're sharing an apartment with a woman here?"

"Yes."

"Someone you've known for some time?"

"Yes, I knew her in Salt Lake City. I've known her for years. We shared an apartment in Salt Lake."

"Telephone?"

"Yes, Gladstone eight-seven-one-nine."

"What's your occupation?"

"I'm a nurse. . . . But wouldn't it be better for me to tell you what I want to see you about, Mr. Mason, before we go into all of these incidental matters?"

Mason shook his head slowly and said, "I always like to get the picture. How did you happen to consult me?"

"I heard you were a very fine lawyer."

"So you came on here from Salt Lake City to see me?"

"Well, not exactly."

"You came by train?"

"No, by plane."

"When?"

"Recently."

"Precisely when did you arrive?"

"At ten o'clock this morning—if you *have* to know."

"Who recommended me to you?"

"A man I knew in Australia."

Mason raised his eyebrows in silent inquiry.

"Bishop Mallory. He wasn't a bishop when I knew him, but he's a bishop now."

"And he suggested you come here?"

"Yes."

"Then you've seen the bishop since your arrival?"

She hesitated and said slowly, "I can't see that that makes any different, Mr. Mason."

Mason smiled and said, "Well, perhaps you're right, particularly since I don't think I'm going to be able to handle your case. You see, I'm very busy with a lot of important matters and . . ."

"Oh, but you *must*. I . . . you'll just *have* to, that's all."

"*When* did you see Bishop Mallory?" Mason asked.

She sighed and said, "A few hours ago."

"But you've been here since morning?"

"Yes."

"Why didn't you come to see me during office hours?"

She shifted her position uneasily. Resentment flared for a moment in her reddish-brown eyes. Then she took a deep breath and said slowly, "Bishop Mallory suggested I come to you. I couldn't see the bishop until a short time ago. He'd been injured and was in a hospital."

"And he suggested you come to me?"

"Yes, of course."

"Did he give you a letter to me?"

"No."

"Then," Mason said, making his tone carry an implied accusation, "you have absolutely nothing to show that you actually know Bishop Mallory, that you actually saw him, or that he suggested you come to me." She fought back resentment in her eyes and shook her head. Mason said, "Under those circumstances I'm quite certain I couldn't interest myself in your problems."

She seemed to debate with herself for a moment, then snapped open the black handbag which had been reposing in her lap. "I think," she said, "this may answer your question." Her gloved fingers fumbled around in the inside of the purse. Mason's eyes suddenly glinted with interest as the lights reflected from the blued steel barrel of an automatic which nestled within the black bag. As though sensing his scrutiny, she pivoted her body in a half-turn so that her shoulder was between Mason's eyes and the bag. Then she pulled out a yellow envelope, took from it a Western Union telegram, carefully snapped the bag shut and handed the telegram to Mason.

The telegram had been sent from San Francisco and was addressed to Julia Branner, care of The Sisters' Hospital, Salt Lake City, Utah, and read simply: MEET ME REGAL HOTEL LOS ANGELES AFTERNOON OF THE FOURTH. BRING ALL DOCUMENTS—WILLIAM MALLORY.

Mason frowned thoughtfully at the telegram and said, "You didn't meet Bishop Mallory this afternoon?"

"No. I told you he'd been injured."

"You saw him this evening, a few hours ago?"

"Yes."

"Did he say anything to you about his future plans?"

"No."

"Just what *did* he say?"

46

"He suggested I should see you and tell you my entire story."

Mason sat back in his swivel chair and said, "Go ahead."

"Do you," she asked, "know of Renwold C. Brownley?"

"I've heard of him," Mason said noncommittally.

"Did you know of an Oscar Brownley?"

"I've heard of him."

"I," she announced, "am Mrs. Oscar Brownley!"

She paused dramatically. Mason took a cigarette from the case on his desk and said, "And you are, I believe, a fugitive from justice under an old felony warrant for manslaughter issued in Orange County."

Her jaw sagged as though he had struck her unexpectedly in the solar plexus. "How . . . how did you know that? The bishop wasn't to tell you that!"

Mason shrugged his shoulders and said, "I merely mentioned it so you'd realize it wouldn't be worthwhile to misrepresent matters to me. Suppose you go ahead and tell me your story and make sure you tell me *all* of it."

She took a deep breath and rushed headlong into an account which poured from her lips with such glib alacrity that it might have been memorized or, on the other hand, might have been the result of long brooding over wrongs. "Twenty-two years ago," she said, "I was wild—plenty wild. Renwold Brownley was in the real estate business and didn't have very much money. Oscar was the apple of his eye, but Oscar liked to step around in the white lights. I was a nurse. I met Oscar at a party. He fell in love with me, and we were married. It was one of those hectic affairs which sometimes happen.

"The old man was furious because we hadn't consulted him; but I think it would have been all right if it hadn't been for the auto accident. That was a mess. We'd had a few drinks but I wasn't drunk. An old man, whose reactions were so sluggish he shouldn't have been driving a car anyway, came around the corner on the wrong side. I tried to avoid him by swinging over sharply to the left. If he'd stayed on his left side, everything would have been all right, but he got rattled and pulled back to the right. As a result, when the accident took place I was apparently entirely in the wrong. I wasn't tight, but I'd been drinking. Oscar was good and tight. That's why I was driving the car.

"You know how they used to be in Orange County. They'd put you in jail for going thirty miles an hour. Oscar made a touch from his dad, and we skipped out. We were going on a honeymoon, anyway. We went to Australia.

"Then was when I got double-crossed and didn't know it. Oscar asked his dad to hush the thing up and make a cash settlement, but, the way it looks now, the old man did just the opposite. It was right about that time he commenced to make money—big money. Oscar was the apple of his eye. He thought that Oscar had thrown himself away on a wild, harum-scarum woman who would have given herself to him or to anyone else without marriage as easily as with marriage. We were in a strange country. I had the very devil of a time getting work. Oscar couldn't get anything. The old man evidently pulled political wires, not to hush the accident up, but to get a manslaughter warrant issued for me so I could never come back. Then he corresponded secretly with Oscar.

"I didn't know all this at the time. I came home one day and found Oscar gone. His father had cabled him money to come home. I worked for a few months after that and then couldn't work any longer until my child was born. Oscar didn't even know about her, and I swore that he never should. I hated him and hated his family and hated all they stood for. At that time I didn't know how much money Renwold Brownley was making. It wouldn't have made much difference if I had. I determined to stand on my own two feet. . . . But I couldn't keep the child, and I was damned if I'd let him have her.

"Bishop Mallory was a rector—Church of England, you know—and one of the most human ministers I've ever known. He didn't have the smug, self-righteous attitude so many preachers have. He was a man who wanted to help people—and he helped me. I confided in him, and one day he came to me and told me he had a chance to get a good home for Janice. He said the people weren't particularly wealthy but they were comfortably situated and could give Janice an education. But they insisted that I must never know who had taken her and must never try to follow her. Bishop Mallory had to promise by everything he held sacred he'd never tell me anything about her or where she was."

"He's kept that promise?" Mason asked.

"Absolutely," Julia Branner said, and there were tears in her eyes. "When we're young we're impulsive. We do things without thinking that we're bound to regret them afterwards. I got married on impulse and I released all claims on my daughter on impulse. I've regretted doing both. . . ." Her lips quivered. She blinked rapidly and said, "Not that it makes a d-d-damned bit of difference—regrets, I mean." She tossed her head and went on, "Don't worry, Mr. Mason, I'm not going to bawl. I've fought my way through life. I've violated damn near all the conventions at one time or another, and I've paid the price. I haven't whimpered and I'm not going to whimper."

"Go on," Mason said.

"After several years I came back to the States. I found that Renwold Brownley was wallowing in money. Apparently Oscar didn't have anything except what Renwold wanted to give him. Naturally, I thought Oscar should do something for me. I got in touch with him. He wrote me a very short letter. So far as he was concerned, I was merely a fugitive from justice. The old man was very bitter. If I returned to California, I'd be prosecuted on that manslaughter charge. . . . Oh, I saw the sketch, all right, but what could *I* do? I was a nurse working for wages. Oscar'd got a divorce on some charge or another. Renwold Brownley had millions. There was a manslaughter warrant out for me. Not that I cared particularly about coming to California. I didn't want Oscar back. I *did* think he might make some sort of settlement, but my hands were tied. The charge against me wasn't just one of drunken driving; it was a manslaughter charge and, with Renwold Brownley's money and political backing against me, I'd have been railroaded to the penitentiary, lost my citizenship, lost my standing as a nurse, lost my ability to earn a living. . . . Anyway, that's the way I felt about it. I was too frightened even to consult a lawyer because I didn't dare to confide in one."

"Go on," Mason said, his voice showing interest.

"The only thing I wanted was to have my daughter get something of what was rightfully hers. So I wrote to Australia. The Reverend William Mallory had become a bishop by that time, but he couldn't give me any help. He reminded me of my promise and of his. My daughter had been taken by people who were good to her. She thought they were her own father and mother. They were so attached to her they'd have died rather than let her think differently. They didn't have any great amount of money but they were fairly well fixed. I learned that my daughter had a natural aptitude for nursing and had wanted to do that more than anything else on earth. She was in a hospital, studying. She wanted to train herself to nurse children—she would. She came by it honestly. Mr. Mason, I moved heaven and earth to find her. I'd made a promise, but what the hell's a promise when it's the case of a mother trying to find her own daughter? I spent every cent I could get, hiring detectives. They couldn't find her. Bishop Mallory had been too smart. He'd covered the trail too well, and he wouldn't talk. And then I got this wire from Bishop Mallory. I thought he was going to tell me everything. My girl is of age now. There's no reason why she shouldn't know, and I think the people who adopted her have died, but the bishop wouldn't tell me anything. He only said I was to see you. But I did find out that after Oscar died, Renwold realized there was a grandchild somewhere, and he'd employed detectives to find her. He'd taken a girl named Janice in to live with him. . . . But . . . Bishop Mallory tells me she isn't the *real* Janice. She's a fraud." She paused, staring with hot, defiant eyes at the lawyer.

"What do you want me to do?" Mason asked.

"Nothing for me, but I want you to rip the mask off of that spurious granddaughter. I want you to find my daughter and see that she's recognized as a Brownley."

"That wouldn't necessarily mean anything," Mason said. "Renwold could make a will disinheriting her. I think there's another grandchild, isn't there—a grandson?"

"Yes, a Philip Brownley. But somehow I think Renwold would never disinherit Janice. I think he'd do something for her."

"And that's all?" Mason asked.

"That's all."

"Nothing for yourself?"

"Not a damned cent. . . . You don't mind my cussing once in a while, do you? It makes me feel better. I've been kicked around and I've found I have to either bawl or cuss. Personally, I prefer to cuss."

Mason regarded her in slow appraisal and suddenly said, "Julia, why are you carrying that gun?"

She grabbed instinctively at the bag in her lap, pushed it to the other side of her body. Mason's eyes bored steadily into hers. "Answer me," he said.

She said slowly, "I had to go back and forth from the hospital at all hours of the night. Some of the nurses were annoyed. The police themselves suggested it would be a good thing for me to carry a gun."

"And you have a permit for it?"

"Yes, of course."

"Why are you carrying it now?"

"I don't know. I've always carried it ever since I bought it. It's become second nature, just like carrying lipstick. I swear that's the only reason, Mr. Mason."

"If," Mason said, "you have a permit to carry that gun, it means that the number is registered with the police. You know that, don't you?"

"Yes, of course."

"Did you," Mason asked, "know that Bishop Mallory sailed very suddenly and unexpectedly on the *Monterey*, leaving his baggage in his room at the Regal Hotel?"

She clamped her lips together in a firm line and said, "I'd prefer not to discuss Bishop Mallory. After all, the question which concerns me relates only to my daughter."

"And when do you want me to start?" Mason asked.

She got to her feet and said, "Right now. I want you to fight that cold-blooded devil until he yells for mercy. I want you to prove that *he* was the one responsible for getting a manslaughter warrant issued for me and keeping me out of the state so he could wreck my marriage and discriminate against my daughter. Not that *I* want a cent, I simply want him licked. I want you to make the old devil realize that money can't buy him immunity to do just as he d-d-damn pleases." There were no tears in her eyes now, but her mouth was writhing. Her hot eyes stared at the lawyer.

Perry Mason regarded her for several long seconds, then picked up the telephone on his desk and said to Della Street, "Call Renwold C. Brownley."

Chapter 6

Midnight rain, lashing down from a sodden sky, and borne on the wings of a whipping south wind, moistened the leaves of the shrubbery about Renwold C. Brownley's Beverly Hills mansion. The headlights of Mason's automobile reflected from the shiny surfaces of the green leaves as his car swung in a skidding turn around the driveway.

The lawyer stopped his car under the protection of a porte-cochere. A butler whose countenance was as uncordial as the weather opened the door and said, "Mr. Mason?"

The lawyer nodded.

"This way," the butler said. "Mr. Brownley is waiting for you." He made no effort to relieve Mason of his coat or hat. He ushered Mason through a reception hall into a huge library paneled with dark wainscoting. Subdued lights illuminated tiers of shelved books, deep chairs, spacious alcoves, inviting window seats.

The man who sat at the massive mahogany table was as unrelentingly austere as some fabled judge of the Inquisition. His hair was white and so fine that the eyebrows were all but invisible, giving to his head a peculiar vulture-like appearance, making his scrutiny seem a lidless, cold survey. "So you're Perry Mason," he said, in a voice which held no trace of welcome. It was the voice of one who is inspecting for the first time an interesting specimen.

Mason shook moisture from his rain coat as he flung it from his shoulders and dropped it uninvited over the back of a chair. Standing with his shoulders squared, feet spread slightly apart, the soft shaded lights of the library illuminating his granite-hard profile and steady, patient eyes, he said, "Yes, I'm Mason, and you're Brownley." And the lawyer contrived to put in his tone exactly that same lack of sympathy which had characterized the voice of the older man.

"Sit down," Brownley said. "In some ways I'm glad you came, Mr. Mason."

"Thanks," Mason told him. "I'll sit down after a while. I prefer to stand right now. Just why is it you're glad I came?"

"You said you wanted to talk with me about Janice?"

"Yes."

"Mr. Mason, you're a very clever lawyer."

"Thank you."

"Don't thank me. I'm not paying you a compliment. It's an admission. Under the circumstances, perhaps, rather a grudging admission. I have followed your exploits in the press with a feeling of amazement. Also with a feeling of curiosity. I'll admit that I've been interested in you, that I've wanted to meet you. In fact, upon one case I even thought of consulting you, but one hardly places matters of, shall we say financial importance, in the hands of an attorney whose forte seems to be mental agility rather than . . ."

"Responsibility?" Mason asked sarcastically as Brownley hesitated.

"No, that isn't what I meant," Brownley said, "but your skill lies along the lines of the spectacular and the dramatic. As you become older, Mr. Mason, you'll find that men who have large interests tend to fight shy of the spectacular and the dramatic."

"In other words, you didn't consult me."

"That's right."

"And since you didn't elect to avail yourself of my services, I am at perfect liberty to offer those services to people who are on the other side."

The ghost of a smile twitched the lips of the man who sat at the mahogany table surrounded by the environments of his wealth, entrenched in an aura of financial power as though it had been a fortress. "Well put," he said. "Your skill in turning my own comments back on me is well in keeping with what I've heard of your talents."

Mason said, "I've explained to you generally over the telephone what brings me here. It's about your granddaughter.

54

Regardless of what you may think, Mr. Brownley, I'm not merely a paid gladiator fighting for those who have the funds with which to employ me. I'm a fighter, yes, and I like to feel that I fight for those who aren't able to fight for themselves, but I don't offer my services indiscriminately. I fight to aid justice."

"Are you asking me, Mr. Mason, to believe that you only seek to right wrongs?" Brownley asked in a thinly skeptical voice.

"I'm not asking you to believe one Goddamn thing," Mason told him. "I'm *telling* you. You can believe it or not."

Brownley frowned. "There's no call to get abusive, Mr. Mason," he said.

"I think," the lawyer told him, "that I'm the best judge of that, Mr. Brownley." And with that he sat down and lit a cigarette, conscious that the super-composure of the financier had been considerably jarred. "Now then," Mason went on, "whenever a man has something which other men want, he's subject to all sorts of pressure. You have money. Other men want it. They try all sorts of schemes to get you to give up that money. I have a certain ability as a fighter and men try to impose upon my credulity in order to enlist my sympathies.

"Now I'm going to put my cards on the table with you. The whole chain of events leading up to my interest in this matter has been very unusual. I'm not certain that it hasn't been an elaborate build-up in order to gain my partisan support. If it has, I don't want to lend any such ability as I may have to perpetrating an injustice or bolstering a fraud. If, on the other hand, the chain of circumstances isn't part of an elaborate stage-setting, but represents a genuine sequence of events, there's a very great possibility that the person whom you believe to be the daughter of your son Oscar and Julia Branner isn't related to you."

"You have some authority for making this assertion?" Brownley asked.

"Naturally." Mason paused to regard the smoldering tip of his cigarette, then, letting his eyes meet the lidless scrutiny of the other man, said, "I have it on the authority of the only surviving parent, Julia Branner herself."

There was no sign of emotion upon Brownley's face. His smile was distinctly frosty. "And may I ask," he inquired, "who in turn has identified Julia Branner?"

Mason held his face in rigid immobility. "No one," he admitted, "and that is why I came to you. If there is any fraud on my side of the case, you are the person to expose it."

"And if I convince you that such fraud exists?" Brownley asked.

Mason made a spreading gesture with his palms and said, "The case will no longer interest me. But understand, Mr. Brownley, I must be convinced."

"Julia Branner," Brownley said, "is an adventuress. My detectives have gathered things concerning her past life before she met my son. It is rather an extraordinary compilation."

Mason conveyed his cigarette to his lips, inhaled deeply, smiled and spoke as he exhaled, the cigarette smoke clothing the words with a smoky aura. "Doubtless," he said, "there are many women whose pasts, if viewed under the microscopes of such investigation, would appear checkered."

"This woman is an adventuress."

"You are referring now to the Julia Branner who married your son?"

"Yes, of course."

"Then," Mason pointed out, "the fact that she is an adventuress has nothing whatever to do with the legal status of the child she bore."

Brownley wet his lips, hesitated a moment, then went on with the cold, relentless manner of a banker analyzing the defects in a financial statement: "Fortunately for all concerned, the child she bore was removed from her influence at an early age. I don't care to divulge exactly how that happened nor where it happened. That information was gathered for me by men who were exclusively and entirely in my employ, and who were actuated solely by a desire to protect my interests. I happen to know, and doubtless you can verify, that Julia Branner herself made futile but nevertheless expensive efforts to secure this same information for herself. It happened that, because of the added facilities at my command, I was successful where she had failed."

"Has Julia ever sought to capitalize upon her connection with your family . . . ? I am asking you now to set aside your prejudices and give me a fair answer."

Brownley's face was grim. "She has never sought to capitalize," he admitted, "because I have forestalled any such effort on her part."

"I take it," Mason said, "you are referring to the fact that you were able to place her in the position of being a fugitive from justice."

"You may interpret my statement any way you wish," Brownley said. "I am making no admissions."

"I think it only fair to warn you that if I interest myself in this case," Mason pointed out, "I shall endeavor to protect the interests of my client all along the line, and if it appears that she became a technical fugitive from justice because of influence which was brought to bear by you, I shall seek to make you pay for having exerted that influence."

"Naturally," Brownley said, "I would hardly expect Perry Mason to fight half-heartedly, but I don't think you are going to interest yourself in Julia Branner's behalf. In the first place, I have every reason to believe that the real Julia Branner is dead, and that *you* are the one who has taken up with an impostor."

"Nothing which you have said," Mason pointed out, "in any way proves that the young woman whom you have recognized as your granddaughter is in fact the daughter of Julia Branner, wherever Julia Branner may be. On the other hand, *I* have some evidence which leads me to believe you have been the victim of either a fraud or a mistake."

Brownley said slowly, "Mr. Mason, I am not going to divulge my defenses to any claims which you may make."

"In that case," the lawyer said emphatically, "you can do nothing to convince me I shouldn't take the case."

Brownley sat for several seconds in frowning concentration. At length he said, "I will go this far and this far alone, Mr. Mason," and his long, thin fingers took a sealskin wallet from his pocket, opened it and extracted a letter. Mason watched the man with interest as he calmly and deliberately tore the printed portion of the letter-head from the stationery and then, after a moment, tore off the signature.

"You will understand, Mr. Mason," Brownley said, fingering the mutilated letter speculatively, "that when I made my investigation I made a most complete investigation. I had certain irrefutable facts which I could use as base lines in making my survey. The nature of those facts are highly confidential, but I employed the best investigators money could buy. I believe you are being victimized. I am morally certain the woman who has presented herself to you as Julia Branner is not the woman who married my son. I *know* that the person who will be produced by her as her child will not be the daughter of my dead son, and I have reason to believe that your own interest in the matter has been excited largely because you feel a certain person whom you consider above reproach, and who *should* be in a position to have accurate information, has interested himself in the person who seeks to become your client. Therefore, I am willing to show you this letter. I will not tell you whom it is from, but will merely state that I consider the source to be above reproach."

Brownley extended the letter. Mason read:

"As a result of our investigation, we feel that we can state definitely an attempt will be made to discredit the real Janice Brownley and substitute in her place an impostor. The parties who will be interested in doing this have been fully conversant with the situation for some months and have been carefully awaiting the most auspicious time to launch their activities. In order to be successful, they will have to interest some attorney of ability who will be able to finance the fight, and in order to convince such an attorney, it will be necessary to have some influence brought to bear upon him.

"These parties deliberately waited until Bishop William Mallory, of Sydney, Australia, took a sabbatical year. He announced his intention to spend this year in travel and study and, to safeguard himself from interruptions, kept his itinerary a closely guarded secret.

"Our investigator has established an inside contact with these parties and we are, therefore, in a position to inform you that a clever impostor will pose as Bishop Mallory, contact some attorney, who has been carefully selected well in

58

advance, and persuade him to act in the matter. This spurious bishop will appear upon the scene only long enough to impress the attorney. He will then disappear.

"We are advising you of this in advance so you may take steps to apprehend this impostor if he remains in contact with the parties long enough to enable you to have a warrant issued. In any event, you may anticipate that some aggressive attorney, of sufficient financial responsibility to handle the case on a contingency basis, will interest himself in the matter. We would suggest you consult with your attorney in order to anticipate this situation and map out your own plan of campaign. We will have additional facts to report within the next few days.

"Very truly yours,"

"Doubtless," Mason said, his face not changing expression by so much as the motion of a muscle, "this letter carries weight with you?"

"It doesn't with *you*?" Brownley asked, watching him shrewdly, his voice showing some surprise.

"None whatever."

"I paid money to get that letter." Brownley said. "When you know me better, Mr. Mason, you'll know that whenever I pay money for anything, I get the best. Permit me to state: That letter carries great weight with me."

"The letter *might* have carried great weight with me," Mason told him, "if I had seen it as a letter. But you chose to tear off everything of value, leaving nothing but an anonymous communication, and I, therefore, regard it as such—merely an anonymous letter."

Brownley's face showed his irritation. "If you think," he said, "that I'm going to divulge the identity of my fact-finding organizations, you're mistaken."

Mason shrugged his shoulders and said, "I think nothing. I merely placed certain cards on the table and asked you to match them. So far you haven't done it."

"And," Brownley announced with finality, "that's just as far as I'm going." Mason pushed back his chair as though to rise. "Not going, Mr. Mason?" Brownley asked.

"Yes. If you have given me all you have to offer, you have fallen far short of convincing me."

"Has it ever occurred to you, Mr. Mason, that *you* are not the one to be convinced?"

Mason, who was standing with his knuckles resting on the edge of the table, the weight of his broad shoulders supported by his rigid arms, said, "No, it hasn't. For the purpose of this interview, I'm the boss. If you can't convince me you're in the right, you've got a fight on your hands."

"Spoken like a good business man," Brownley conceded. "But I'm going to show that you're checkmated before you start."

"Checkmated," Mason said, "is an expression of considerable finality. I have been in 'check' many times; I have been checkmated but seldom."

"Nevertheless," Brownley said, "you're checkmated now. It happens, Mr. Mason, that I don't want my granddaughter's name dragged through a lot of court proceedings. I don't want a lot of newspaper notoriety focused upon my private affairs. Therefore, I am going to keep you from engaging in any fight for this spurious grandchild."

Despite himself, Mason's voice showed surprise. "*You're* going to keep *me* from doing something *I* want to do?" he asked.

"Exactly," Brownley said.

"It *has* been tried before," Mason told him dryly, "but never with any great degree of success."

Brownley's lidless eyes twinkled with frosty merriment. "I can well understand that, Counselor," he said, "but since you have investigated my family, you may have investigated me, and if so, you have doubtless learned that I am a ruthless fighter, a hard man to cross, and one who *always* gets his own way."

"You are now speculating," Mason said, "upon the outcome. Your statement a moment ago was to the effect that you were going to keep me from *starting* proceedings."

"I am."

Mason's smile of polite incredulity was a sufficient comment in itself.

60

"I am going to keep you from doing it," Brownley said, "because you are a businessman. The other side have no funds with which to fight. Their only hope lies in interesting some attorney who has ample finances of his own, who will be willing to gamble upon a contingency. Therefore, if I can show you that you have no hope of winning, you are a good enough business man not to start."

"It would," Mason told him, "take a mighty good man to convince me I had no hope of winning a lawsuit. I prefer to reach my own conclusions on that."

"Understand," Brownley said, "I am not foolish enough to think that I could prevent you from seeking to establish the legitimacy of a spurious grandchild, but I do feel certain that I can show you it won't do you any good when once you have established your claim. Being my grandchild means nothing to anyone. The girl is of age and under any circumstances there would be no obligation on my part to support her. The sole advantage to be derived from establishing the relationship would be the expectancy of sharing in my property after I have gone. Therefore, Mr. Mason, I am making a will in which the bulk of my property is left to my granddaughter, Janice Brownley, and I particularly provide in that will that the person to whom I refer as my granddaughter is the one who is at present living with me as my grandchild; that it makes no difference whether the relationship is authentic or not; that *she* is the beneficiary under my will. Now then, I know that you *might* try to set such a will aside. Therefore, tomorrow morning at nine o'clock I shall sign conveyances which will irrevocably convey to the person who is living with me as my granddaughter a full three-fourths of my property, reserving a life estate to myself. The remaining one-fourth will be similarly transferred to my other grandchild, Philip Brownley."

Brownley's steady, cold eyes stared triumphantly at the lawyer. "Now, Counselor," he went on, "there is a perfectly impossible legal nut for you to crack. I think you are too smart a man to butt your head against a brick wall. I want you to understand that in me you have found an adversary as ruthless as yourself. There's nothing at which I will stop when I have once made up my mind. In that way, I am, I think, much like yourself. But it happens that in this matter I hold *all* of the trump cards, and I intend to play them with every bit of cold-blooded efficiency at my command. And now, Mr. Mason, let me wish you good night and tell you that I have enjoyed meeting you." Renwold Brownley wrapped long fingers about Mason's muscular hand, and Mason found those fingers as cold as steel.

"The butler," Brownley said, "will show you to your car." And the butler, doubtless summoned by some secret signal, noiselessly opened the library door and bowed to Perry Mason.

Mason stared at Brownley. "You're not a lawyer?" he asked.

"No, but I have the benefit of the best legal talent available."

Mason turned, nodded to the butler and picked up his rain coat. "When I have finished with the case," he said grimly, "you *may* have changed your mind about the efficiency of your lawyers. Good night, Mr. Brownley."

Mason paused at the outer door long enough to let the butler assist him into his coat. Rain was beating down in torrents, whipping the surface of the driveway into miniature geysers. The branches of the wind-lashed trees tossed about like grotesque arms, waving in surrender to the storm. Mason slammed the door of his car, switched on the ignition and headlights, snapped the gearshift back into low gear, and eased in the clutch. The car purred out from the shelter of the porte-cochere into the full force of the storm. He had shifted to second, and was placing a cautious foot upon the brake pedal to slow down for a curve in the graveled driveway, when his headlights picked out a figure which stood, braced against the beating rain.

Against the black background of the shrubbery, the figure was etched into white brilliance by the headlights, a slender young man, a rain coat turned up about his neck, a hat pulled low down on the forehead, water streaming from the brim. He extended his arms, and Mason kicked out the clutch and slowed the car to a stop. The young man walked toward him.

Mason was conscious of the white pallor of the face, of the

burning purpose in the dark eyes. Mason rolled down the window of his car.

"You're Mr. Mason, the lawyer?" the young man asked.

"Yes."

"I'm Philip Brownley. Does that mean anything to you?"

"Grandson of Renwold Brownley?" Mason asked.

"Yes."

"And you wanted to see me?"

"Yes."

"Better get in out of the rain," Mason said. "Perhaps you'd like to drive to my office with me."

"No. And my grandfather mustn't know that I've talked with you. Tell me, you talked with him?"

"Yes."

"What about?"

"I'd prefer that you made your inquiries from your grandfather," Mason said.

"It was about Jan, wasn't it?"

"Jan?"

"You know, Janice—my cousin."

"After all," Mason told him, "I don't feel free to discuss the matter, particularly at present."

"I might make you a valuable ally," Philip offered.

"You might," Mason admitted.

"After all, our interests are somewhat in common."

"Do you mean by that," Mason inquired, "that you feel the person living here in the house as Janice Brownley isn't the daughter of Oscar Brownley?"

"I meant," Philip repeated, "that I might make you an ally."

Mason said slowly, "I don't think there's anything I'd care to discuss with you at present."

"Is it true that Grandfather is going to tie your hands by conveying all of his property to Janice and reserving only a life estate for himself?"

"That's also something I'd prefer not to discuss right now. But I'd like very much to talk with you at a more propitious time. Suppose you come to my office tomorrow morning at about ten o'clock."

"No! No! I can't. But don't you understand what's happened? Grandfather hired a firm of detectives to find Janice. He offered a bonus of twenty-five thousand dollars if they'd find her. They couldn't find Janice, but they weren't going to pass up twenty-five thousand dollars, so they faked the whole business. She's been living here for two years and she's hypnotized him utterly and completely. Morally, I'm entitled to just as much of the estate as she is, even if she's genuine. But she's hypnotized him into giving her the bulk of the property. She's an unscrupulous, scheming adventuress. She wouldn't stop at anything. She . . ." Philip Brownley's voice choked with indignation. For several seconds the only sounds were those of the storm, the rain drumming on the roof of the closed car, the tossing branches of the trees, the rush of the wind.

Mason, staring steadily at the young man, said, "So what?"

"I want you to stop it."

"How?"

"I don't know how. That's up to you. I just want you to know you can count on my support—but it must be secret. Grandfather must never know it."

"Can you come to my office?" Mason asked.

"No. He'd find it out."

"How do you know she's a fake?"

"The way she's gone about wheedling her way into his affections."

"That's not evidence."

"There are other things."

Mason said, "Look here, young man, when you first talked about her, you referred to her as 'Jan.' That's sort of a pet name. Now you *may* be trying to help me, and you *may* be trying to pump me to find out what I plan on doing. I've offered you a chance to come to my office with me. You won't. You won't even meet me. You can't tell me your grandfather keeps you under such close supervision. Moreover, anyone who might be watching from that house can see I've stopped my car to talk with you. . . ."

"Good Lord!" the young man interrupted, "I never thought of *that*!" He whirled and dove for the shadows of a hedge.

Mason waited a few minutes, then kicked the car into gear

and stepped on the throttle. He drove directly to a branch office of the Western Union. Standing at the counter, with rain trickling down from the skirts of his coat, he wrote a message to be sent by wireless: BISHOP WILLIAM MALLORY S.S. "MONTEREY" EN ROUTE TO SYDNEY AUSTRALIA VIA HONOLULU—IMPORTANT DEVELOPMENTS MAKE IT IMPERATIVE YOU VOUCH FOR IDENTITY OF WOMAN CLAIMING TO BE JULIA BRANNER WHO CALLED ON ME THIS EVENING SHORTLY AFTER YOUR BOAT SAILED.

He signed the message, paid the charges, and stepped into the telephone booth, where he closed the door and called the number Julia Branner had given him. A woman's voice, thin, toneless, and self-effacing, answered the telephone. "Is this Julia Branner?" Mason asked.

"No. This is her friend, Stella Kenwood. Is this Mr. Mason, the lawyer?"

"Yes."

"Just a moment, Mr. Mason. She'll talk with *you*."

After the thin, reedy voice of Stella Kenwood, Julia Branner's resonant, throaty tones seemed to flow over the wire and fill the confines of the telephone booth, in which the warmth of Mason's body, evaporating the moisture from his woolen garments, made the atmosphere close and stuffy. "What did you find out?" she demanded. "Tell me quickly!"

Mason said, "Nothing encouraging. Brownley's a man of considerable determination. He's planning to make a will leaving the bulk of his property to the girl who's been living there in the house as his granddaughter. He's also planning to convey her most of his property outright, leaving only a life estate in himself."

"He's done that already?" Julia Branner said.

"No. He's going to do it in the morning."

Mason could hear her inhale a quick breath. "Is there anything we can do between now and morning?" she asked.

"No," he said. "Unless we could show he was incompetent, we couldn't stop him from doing as he pleased with his property at any time he pleased. But we have a remedy he hasn't thought of. I'll explain it to you in the morning."

There were several moments of silence during which Mason

could hear only the buzzing of the wire. Then Julia Branner's voice said, "Do you think there's anything you can do, Mr. Mason?"

"I'll talk it over with you in the morning," he said.

"It sounds very discouraging to me," she insisted. "I think he has us licked, unless . . ."

"Unless what?" Mason asked, after she became silent.

"Unless I do something that I didn't intend to do except as a last resort."

"What?" he asked.

"I think I have one way of convincing Renwold Brownley," she said. "It all depends on whether he wants something which I have badly enough to do exactly what I tell him to."

Mason said, "Now, listen. You keep out of this and sit tight. I'll talk with you in the morning. You can't force Brownley to do anything. He's shrewd, obstinate, and ruthless." When there was no answer to what he had said, Mason tapped the transmitter with his knuckles and said, "Did you hear me?"

"Yes. I heard you," she said in a noncommittal tone. "What time can I see you in the morning?"

"Ten o'clock," he told her, "at my office," and hung up the receiver.

Chapter 7

Rain was beating with steady insistence against the windows of Perry Mason's apartment when he was awakened by the steady ringing of the telephone. He groped for the switch of his bed lamp, propped himself up in bed and lifted the receiver to his ear. The damp breeze which came in through the open window and whipped the lace curtains in flapping protest against the wet screens, blew cold across the lawyer's chest. He groped for his bathrobe and was pulling it up under his chin as he said, "Hello," and heard Paul Drake's voice saying, "Here's a break, Perry. It looks as though you've drawn another one." Mason rubbed sleep from his eyes and said thickly, "What's happened? What time is it?"

"It's exactly three-fifteen," Drake said. "One of my men has telephoned from Wilmington. You wanted the Brownley angle covered, so I put a shadow out at the house. About an hour ago old Brownley climbed into his coupe and started going places. It was raining hard. My man followed. He tagged along without any difficulty until Brownley got down to the harbor district. He figured Brownley was heading straight for the yacht he keeps. So my man got just a little careless. He let Brownley get too far ahead of him and lost him, figured there was nothing to it, went over to the yacht and waited. Brownley didn't show up. My man started making a swing around, trying to find the car. He'd been driving around about ten minutes when he saw a man running and waving his arms. My man stopped the car. This chap ran up to him and said that Brownley had been murdered; that some woman in a white rain coat had stepped out of the shadows, climbed onto the running board of Brownley's car, fired five or six shots, and then beat it.

"This guy was pretty rattled. He wanted to telephone

headquarters right away. My operative ran him to a telephone, and they called the ambulance and the police, although this witness insisted the man was so dead there was no use getting an ambulance. After they'd telephoned, my operative went back to find the car and the body. They couldn't find it. The police showed up and *they* couldn't find it. I'm going down to look the situation over and I figured you might like to come along."

"It was Renwold C. Brownley?" Mason asked.

"In person."

"That," the lawyer said, "is going to make a splash."

"Are you telling me?" Drake said. "Every newspaper in the city will be getting out extras within the next two hours."

"Where are you now?"

"At my office."

"Drive down for me and I'll be dressed and standing on the sidewalk by the time you get here," Mason said.

He hung up the telephone, jumped out of bed and closed the window with his right hand while he was unbuttoning his pajamas with his left. Mason tied his necktie in the elevator, struggled into his rain coat as he crossed the lobby of the apartment house, and reached the pavement just as Drake's automobile slewed around the corner, sending the twin beams of dazzling headlights dancing through the rain, illuminating the little mushrooms of water which geysered up from the wet pavement as the big drops bulleted downward. As Drake skidded the car away from the curb, Mason settled himself against the cushions and said, "A woman did the killing, Paul?"

"Yes, a woman in a white rain coat."

"What happened?"

"As nearly as I could get it over the telephone, Brownley was looking for someone. He had slowed his car almost to a stop and was crawling along the pavement when this woman stepped out from the deeper shadows. He had evidently been expecting her because he stopped his coupe and rolled down the window. She climbed up on the running board, raised an automatic, and fired a bunch of shots. Then she jumped back to the street, sprinted around the corner, and made a get-away.

68

The witness saw the get-away car. It was a Chevrolet, but he couldn't get the license number. He took a look in the coupe and saw Brownley all in a huddle against the steering wheel. Apparently every one of the shots had taken effect. The witness started to run without any very definite objective. He said he'd run for four or five minutes when he saw the headlights of my operative's machine."

"Some chance he was confused in his directions?" Mason asked.

"Every chance on earth. It's a ten to one bet that he was."

Drake pushed the throttle down close to the floorboards and said, "Are you nervous, Perry?"

"Go to it," Mason told him. "Don't hesitate on my account. How are your tires?"

"Swell," Drake said, grinning. "According to my theory, a skid is simply an attempt on the part of the hind end to catch up with the front end. If you keep the front end going fast enough, the hind end can't catch up until you try to stop."

Mason lit a cigarette and said, "Have you ever made your will, Paul?"

"Not yet."

"Well, you'd better stop in in the morning and have me draw up one for you. What did you hear about the bishop?"

Drake said, "I guess my Australian agency must have thought I was giving them a bit of leg pulling, or whatever you call it on that side of the water. They sent me back a cable in answer to my inquiry which said simply, 'Bishops seldom stutter.'"

Mason said, "Of course that doesn't answer the question. How about a description of the bishop? Did you get that?"

"Yes, in another cable."

Drake fumbled in his inside pocket, driving with one hand, pulled out a cablegram and handed it across to Mason when the lawyer yelled, "Watch that turn!"

Drake dropped the cablegram, grabbed the steering wheel and fought against the skid as the car lurched into a sickening swing. He spun the wheel hard to the left without effect. A great wave of water was thrown up by the wheels on the right-hand side of the car. Suddenly the front wheels caught. The car snapped into a turn in the opposite direction as Drake spun the steering wheel as though it had been the steering wheel of a yacht. He gave the car the gas as it careened around to the right. The turn loomed in front of the headlights. They swept into it sideways, then the wheels gathered traction. As the car shot for the side of the road, Drake fought it under control just before the front wheels hit the soft shoulder. "Where's the cablegram?" the detective asked. "You didn't drop it, did you?"

Mason sighed, relaxed his legs, which had been braced against the floorboards, and said, "No, it's down here on the seat somewhere."

The detective straightened the car out of the turn, pushed down on the foot throttle, and said, "Can you read it by the dash light?"

Mason said, "I guess so, if my hand will quit jiggling. For God's sake, Paul, don't you ever show any discretion?"

Drake said, "Sure. I was driving all right, but you distracted my attention asking about that cablegram."

Mason unfolded the cablegram and read: BISHOP WILLIAM MALLORY FIFTY-FIVE STOP FIVE FEET SIX STOP WEIGHT ONE HUNDRED SEVENTY-FIVE STOP GRAY EYES STOP HABITUAL PIPESMOKER STOP TAKING SABBATICAL YEAR AND REPORTED BE SOMEWHERE IN UNITED STATES BUT IMPOSSIBLE OBTAIN ACCURATE INFORMATION AS YET STOP

Mason folded the cablegram.

"What do you think of it?" Drake asked.

Mason lit a cigarette. "Go right ahead, Paul, and drive the car. I don't want to distract your attention again. I'll talk with you when we get to where we're going." He settled down against the cushions, pulled the collar of his coat about his neck, dropped his chin on his chest, and smoked in silence.

"The description fits him right enough, doesn't it?" Drake asked. Mason said nothing. Drake chuckled and concentrated upon driving the car. Rain lashed the windshield and drummed on the hood, ran in streams from the glass and metal, showed in driving slants against the illumination of the headlights. The windshield wiper beat monotonously back and forth, but the downpour discounted the rubber-bladed pendulum, distorting the strip of wet pavement gleaming ahead of them.

At length they saw the tail light of an automobile. The headlights of Drake's car picked up a signboard bearing the insignia of a yacht club and the words *"Private, Keep Out."* A man, wearing a rubber rain coat which glistened in the headlights, and from which water ran in rivulets, splashed his way over toward the car.

"You know Mason, Harry," Drake said.

Mason nodded and said, "Hello, Harry. What's new?"

The operative thrust his head through the window of the car. Water from his hat dripped into Drake's lap. Drake yelled, "Take off that hat, you big baboon! Get in the back seat if you want to talk. I don't want a shower bath until morning."

The operative climbed into the back of the car. "Now, listen," he said in a low, rumbling voice of one who is imparting an air of mystery to an important disclosure, "get this straight. It sounds nutty to me. I went out to Brownley's house like you said. It was raining to beat hell. I figured it was just a routine assignment. I couldn't see a millionaire splashing around on a night like this. So I turned up the windows in my car and made myself comfortable. About half past one o'clock a taxicab drove up. Lights went on in the house and I heard a pow-wow. Then the taxicab left, but more lights kept coming on in the house. About fifteen minutes later, lights went on in the garage. Then the garage doors opened and I saw headlights. I managed to get a look at the car as it went past. Old Brownley was driving."

"It was raining all the time?" Drake asked.

"Cats and dogs."

"And Brownley didn't have a chauffeur?" Mason inquired.

"No, he was all alone."

"Go ahead," Drake instructed.

"I followed Brownley, with my lights out part of the time. It was hard going. I didn't dare to crowd him too close. He was pretty much ahead of me by the time we got down here. When he got this far, I figured of course he was going to his yacht, so when he took a turn and acted as though he'd seen me and was trying to shake me off, I beat it directly to the Yacht Club.

After a few minutes, when he didn't show up, I started looking around. I didn't get anywhere. I guess I must have put in five or ten minutes cussing myself and trying to pick up the trail of that car. I took all crossroads, went down by the docks, and had turned back when I saw a man running through the rain and waving his arms. I stopped, and this guy was so excited he could hardly talk.''

"Did you get his name?" Drake asked.

"Yeah, sure I got his name. It was Gordon Bixler.''

"He the chap who told you about the shooting?" Mason asked.

"Yes.''

"What did he say?" Drake wanted to know.

"Wait a minute," Mason said. "We have the highlights on that, but what *I* want to know is what this chap was doing down here. *That* sounds fishy to me.''

"He's okay," the operative said. "I checked on his story. He's a yachtsman who was coming in from Catalina. He was delayed by the storm and had telephoned for his Filipino boy to meet him with a car. The boy evidently didn't like the rain, or was playing around, because he didn't show up, and Bixler, mad as hell, was starting to walk to some place where he could either get a taxi or a telephone. I made him show me his driving license and his cards, and give me the name of his yacht. The cops also checked up on him.''

"Okay," Mason said, "I just wanted to know. Go ahead and give us the dope.''

"Well, Bixler said he'd seen a big coupe come crawling along slowly, as though the guy who was driving it was looking for someone. Then a jane in a white rain coat flagged the coupe and it slowed down. The jane climbed on the running board, apparently talking to the driver, giving him some directions. Then she jumped off the running board and ran back into the shadows by one of the docks. The car drove slowly on. Bixler saw the bird turn down a side street, cross over to another road, speed up, and then make a turn and come back around down the same street.

"Bixler figured this guy might give him a lift, so he stood out in the middle of the street. The car came along, still running about ten or fifteen miles an hour, and then the woman in the white rain coat ran out in front of the headlights and flagged it to a stop again. Bixler started toward the car. He said it was about fifty yards away. The woman in the rain coat stood on the running board and, all of a sudden, Bixler saw flashes and heard an automatic go Bang! Bang! Bang! Bang! He can't be certain whether it was five shots or six, but he thinks it was five. The woman in the rain coat jumped down off the running board and started to sprint for a spur track where the road runs into one of the docks. Bixler waited a minute and then ran toward the coupe. Before he got to the car, he saw a light sedan—he thinks it was a Chevrolet, but he isn't certain—and he *thinks* the driver was the woman in the white rain coat, but he can't be too certain of that. Anyway, the car went out with a roar and the rain swallowed up the tail light in nothing flat.

"Bixler reached the coupe. The driver had slumped over against the door on the left of the car. His arm, shoulder and head were hanging out, with blood streaming down the side of the car to the running board. Bixler says it was Renwold Brownley and that he was pumped full of lead—as dead as a mackerel."

"How does he know it was Brownley?" Mason asked.

"I went into that with him, too. You see, this guy's a yachtsman, and Brownley's a yachtsman. They'd met once or twice at dinners at the Yacht Club, and Bixler had seen Brownley around the Club on half a dozen occasions. He swears there was no chance that he was mistaken; that the man was Brownley. It had been raining hard, but there was a little let-up in the rain about the time of the shooting, and a floodlight from the Yacht Club gave some illumination, and then there was the light from the dashboard in the coupe."

"Then what happened?" Drake asked.

"Bixler started running, looking for a telephone or help of some kind. And I figured he was plenty rattled. He ran along the boulevard for a ways, then he went down to the car track, ran along it for a while, got mixed up on some sidings, came stumbling back, and saw my headlights. He said that must have been about five or ten minutes after the shooting. I picked him up, and he was rattled, so nervous he could hardly talk. He tried to direct me back to the place where the shooting had taken place and couldn't find it. We drove around and around, and I thought the bird was nuts. I'd have passed it all off as a pipe dream if I hadn't been trailing old Renwold Brownley myself and known that he must have been *somewhere* around.

"So this bird kept yelping he wanted to telephone the police, and I figured I might not be in so good with the law if I kept running around in circles, so I ran him up to a telephone and we called the cops."

"Then what happened?" Mason asked.

"The cops showed up and listened to what we had to say and . . ."

"You didn't tell 'em you'd been tailing Brownley, did you?" Drake interrupted.

"Not a chance," the man said scornfully as though resenting the question. "I said I was just driving along, trying to find a party who was on a yacht. I said I was working on a divorce case."

"They ask you who the party was, or anything of that sort?"

"Not yet. They will later. They were too busy then. I let on she was a blonde."

"Could the police find the car?"

"No. Now this is the funny thing: They figured, and I figured, that this guy Bixler was all mixed up and confused and just hadn't pointed out the right spot, but then one of the cops, prowling around with a flashlight, saw a reddish stain in the rain water on the pavement at almost the exact spot where Bixler said he'd seen the shooting. They kept looking around, and picked up a .32 automatic cartridge. You know, one of the empty shells which had been ejected from the gun. That made things look different. It was still raining, but not as hard as it is now, and they were able to follow the little pools of red-tinted water in the surface of the road. The road's a little rough, and there was enough rain to wash blood from the running board of the car to the surface of the road, but not enough to wash away all the stains. The trail pointed in the direction of one of the docks, and they're figuring the car might have been run off the dock."

Mason said, "Where is this dock?"

"Drive on," the detective told them, "and I'll show you. I was just waiting here until you showed up, because this was the place I'd said I'd meet you. Go straight ahead until I tell you to turn."

Drake eased the car into motion, ran for several hundred yards and then the detective said, "Turn to the right here."

As soon as Drake turned, he encountered a string of parked automobiles. Several flood-lights gave a dazzling illumination. A portable searchlight had its beam focused on the water. A wrecking car, equipped with derrick and windlass, was parked at the edge of the wharf. The drums were winding slowly on a taut cable which stretched down into the darkness. From the flattened springs of the wrecking automobile, it was apparent it was lifting some heavy weight. Drake ran the car as far as he could, stopped and said to the operative, "Find a parking place, Harry. Come on, Perry."

The lawyer was already out in the rain. Together, the two men sloshed through the moisture underfoot. Sheeted rain lashed their faces. They joined a small knot of men who were clustered about a corner of the wharf, too engrossed in what they were watching to notice the two newcomers.

Mason peered over the edge. The cable, taut as a bowstring, stretched down into the inky waters, the blackness of which was intensified by the glare of light which beat down through the rain-filled darkness, etching the tense faces of the spectators into a white brilliance. The power-driven winches of the huge wrecking car moved regularly. Occasionally the cable gave forth little snapping noises and sent showers of water spattering from its oily surface.

A man's voice yelled, "There she comes!"

A photographer pushed past Mason and pointed a camera downward. A flashlight puffed blinding illumination into the lawyer's eyes as the top of a coupe moved slowly upward from the rain-lashed waters. Men crowded and jostled. Someone yelled, "Don't raise it any farther until we get another hook on it! It'll weigh more when it gets out of the water. We can't afford to have it break loose."

Men in overalls, with grease-stained faces glistening in the searchlights, sunk a grappling hook into position. From somewhere on the wharf a donkey engine coughed into rhythmic explosions. A derrick arm swung outward. More flashlight photographs were taken. A voice yelled, "Go ahead!" Slowly, the coupe was raised, until it was entirely clear of the water. The right-hand door was jammed wide open. Water seeped out through the cracks in the floorboards, to strike the surface of the bay in splashing rivulets. The man who was in charge yelled, "We're going to raise it with this derrick and swing it inboard. Everyone look out!"

Mason was conscious of a long derrick arm which appeared in the darkness over his head. He saw rope slings being thrown under the body of the car, then winches rattled, a new cable snapped taut as it took up the strain, and the coupe was raised above his head and swung in over the wharf. Just as the car was about to be lowered, a uniformed policeman roped off a space, and the winchmen lowered the coupe within this roped enclosure.

Mason pushed against the rope, peered over the shoulder of an officer whose wet rubber rain coat rubbed against his chin. He saw policemen inspecting the interior of the car, heard one of them yell, "Here's the gun, a .32 automatic. There's still blood left on the seats." There was, Mason saw, no trace of a body.

Someone said, "Get the people off the wharf. Don't let anyone through unless he has proper credentials."

New cars had been arriving. Mason saw a uniformed man bearing down upon him. An officer's rain-spattered face grinned cheerfully as he said with firm insistence, "Go on, buddy, get back off the wharf. You can read about it in the papers." Mason permitted himself to be shoved toward the far end of the wharf. As he passed Paul Drake, he said, "Flash your badge, Paul, and try to get an earful. I'll wait in the car."

The lawyer walked through the driving rain until he found Drake's car, shook what moisture he could from his coat, and climbed into the interior, still steamy with the odors of human occupancy.

Five minutes later, Drake showed up and said, "Not a chance. They're searching for the body. It must have spilled out of the car. There's a bottle of whiskey in that side pocket, Perry."

"My God," Mason said, "never mind the body—why didn't you tell me about the whiskey sooner?" He pulled out the flask, uncorked it and passed it to Drake. "Age before beauty," he said.

Drake took three big gulps, passed the bottle back to Mason, who raised it to his lips and lowered it as Drake's operative came toward the car, the water in his shoes making an audible *squish, squish* with every step.

"Have a drink," Mason said, "and tell us what's new. Could you get anywhere with your badge, Paul?"

"They laughed at me," the detective said. "Then some hard-boiled dick wanted to know what *my* interest in the case was and whom I was representing, how long I'd been there, and what I knew about it and how I happened to be there. I figured it was a good time to beat it. How about you, Harry? What did you find out?"

The rubber-coated detective swiped the back of his hand across his lips and said, "I didn't try to force things any, but just stuck around and picked up a word here and there. I found out that it was Brownley's car, all right. The gearshift showed the car was in low gear when it went over the edge of the wharf, and the hand throttle was pulled wide open."

"The *hand* throttle?" Mason asked.

"That's right. They got the gun, and recovered a couple of bullets which had stuck in the cushions of the front seat. They figured one of the car doors was open when it took the plunge and the body spilled out. They're sending for divers and are going to search the bottom of the bay."

"Any better description of that woman than that she wore a white rain coat?"

"No description that's worth a damn," Harry said. "But they got the number on the gun, and they think they can tell more when they find the body. That taxicab driver evidently took some message to Brownley. Whatever was in the message made him excited as the very devil. It was urgent enough to bring him down here on the run, alone—and it would take something to do that to Renwold C. Brownley at two o'clock in the morning on a night like this."

Drake said, "I'll say so. . . . Let's finish up that bottle of whiskey."

Mason said, "Naughty, naughty, Paul. *You're* driving. Harry and I will finish it."

Chapter 8

The first faint rays of dawn were turning the street into a drab, rain-lashed canyon as Perry Mason parked his car across the street from a three-story frame stucco building which bore the name "Sunset Arms Apartments—214 West Beechwood." Mason turned up the collar of his rain coat and stepped out into the downpour. No lights were showing in the front of the building, but Mason reconnoitered to find an oblong of illumination half screened by lace curtains on the third floor at the back of the building. He walked to the entrance of the apartment house, tried the outer door and found that it was locked; but the well-worn slot for the key readily admitted the blade of Mason's penknife and, under a gentle pressure, the bolt clicked back and the door opened. Mason shook his rain coat and climbed the stairs. His feet squished water from his shoes at every step.

On the third floor he could hear a sound of snoring from one of the apartments, the beat of rain on the roof, the sound of wind moaning around the corners of the building. He walked the length of the corridor and tapped gently on the door from beneath which appeared a faint ribbon of golden light. A woman's voice, sounding thin and frightened, said, "What is it?"

"A message from Miss Branner," Mason said.

There were several seconds of silence while the woman on the other side of the door seemed to be debating whether to accept this statement at its face value. Then Mason heard the sound of shuffling motion, and a bolt clicked back. A thin woman, clad in dressing gown and slippers, her hair done up in curlers, her somewhat sallow face devoid of make-up, contemplated Mason with anxious eyes.

"May I come in?" Mason asked.

She stood in the doorway saying nothing, watching him with a strained anxiety which showed only too well the state of her mind.

Mason laughed reassuringly and said, "After all, you know, I can't give this message to the whole apartment house, and I'm afraid the walls of this corridor are rather thin."

The woman said tonelessly, "Come in."

"I am wondering," Mason said, as he entered the room, "if you're the woman to whom I was to give the message. Would you mind telling me just who you are?"

"If Julia Branner gave you a message," the woman said, "it's for me. I'm Stella Kenwood."

"Oh, yes," Mason said, "you've known Miss Branner for some time, haven't you?"

"Yes."

"Know anything about her past?"

"I know all about it."

"For how far back?"

"Ever since she came to the States."

"Know anything about her life in Australia?"

"Some. Why do you ask?"

"Because," Mason said, "I'm trying to help Miss Branner, and I'll want you to help me, and for that I'll have to know just exactly how well you know her."

"If she gave you a message for me," Stella Kenwood said, making an attempt to assert herself, "you can give it to me. There's no need for any questions."

"Unfortunately," Mason said, "the situation isn't quite that simple. You see, I'm afraid Julia's in trouble."

She gave a quick gasping intake of her breath, then sat down in a chair and said weakly, "Oh."

Mason made a quick survey of the apartment. It was a single-room affair with what was evidently a wall bed on the side to the left of the door. It was a bed which pivoted on a mirrored doorway, and now the full-length mirror was in place, indicating either that the bed had not been slept in or that the woman had arisen, made the bed and raised it into place before Mason had knocked. The apartment was heated by a gas heater molded in the form of a steam radiator covered with aluminum paint, but containing no vent. The atmosphere of the room was warm, steamy and devitalized. Coming in from the open air, Mason was keenly conscious of the close, stale atmosphere. Moisture filmed the windows and the mirror.

"Had the radiator going all night?" he asked.

The woman said nothing, but stared at him with faded blue eyes in which her anxiety showed all too plainly. She was, Mason decided, somewhere in the late forties. Life had not been particularly kind to her, and under the impact of adversity she had learned to turn the other cheek until her manner showed an utter non-resistance.

"What time did Miss Branner leave here?" Mason asked.

"Who are you, and why do you want to know?"

"I'm trying to help her."

"That's what *you* say."

"It's the truth."

"Who are you?"

"I'm Perry Mason."

"The lawyer she went to see?"

"Yes."

"Then I answered you when you called on the telephone last night?"

"Yes."

She nodded without any particular emphasis.

"Where's Julia now?"

"She went out."

"She went out right after I telephoned, didn't she?"

"Not *right* afterwards."

Mason stared steadily at her and she avoided his eyes. "When *did* she go out?" Mason asked.

"Not until around quarter past one o'clock."

"Where did she go?"

"I don't know."

"How did she go?"

"In my car. I gave her the key to it."

"What kind of a car is it?"

"A Chevrolet."

"What did she go out for?"

"I don't think," Stella Kenwood said, "that I should be

talking to you like this." But her voice failed to carry conviction and Mason merely waited expectantly. "You know something, don't you?" she went on. "Something's happened. You're keeping it from me. Tell me."

Mason pressed his advantage by saying, "I'll tell you what's happened as soon as I know how you stand. I can't tell that until after you've answered my questions. Why did Julia go out? What did she want?"

"I don't know."

"Did she have her gun with her?"

The woman gasped, placed a thin hand to her throat. The blue veins showed in a corrugated network over the skin.

"*Did* she have her gun?" Mason repeated.

"I don't know. Why, what's happened? How did *you* know about her gun?"

"Never mind that. Answer my questions. You stayed here waiting for her?"

"Yes."

"Why didn't you go to bed?"

"I don't know. I was worried about her. I kept thinking she'd be coming in."

"Do you know why she came out here from Salt Lake?"

"Yes, of course."

"Why?"

"You know. Why should I tell you?"

"I want to see if she told you the same thing she did me."

"If you're her lawyer, you'd ought to know."

"I know I should," Mason said grimly. "Why did she come?"

"About her daughter and her marriage."

"You know that?"

"Oh, of course."

"How long have you known about it?"

"For some time."

"Julia Branner told you about her marriage to Oscar Brownley?"

"Yes, of course." The woman seemed to warm to her subject. "You see," she said, with the first sign of spontaneity she had shown, "we lived together in Salt Lake three years

82

ago. She told me all about Oscar Brownley, all about the tricks the old man played getting Oscar away from her, and all about how she'd fixed things so the old man could never steal her daughter. You see, I had a daughter of my own just about the same age as Julia's girl, and I could appreciate how she felt. Only, of course, I knew where my daughter was. I could write to her and see her once in a while. Julia didn't even know whether her daughter was still alive. . . ." Her face clouded as she averted her eyes and said, "My daughter died since then, a couple of years ago. So now I know just how Julia must have felt, not being able to see or hear from her loved one."

"Did Julia tell you why she couldn't come back to California?" Mason asked.

"Yes."

"Why?"

"Because of the manslaughter charge."

"All right," Mason said, "let's get down to brass tacks. I want to know why Julia sent a message to Brownley to meet her down at the waterfront."

Stella Kenwood shook her head blankly.

"Don't know?" Mason asked.

"I don't want to talk with you about Julia's affairs."

"You *do* know," Mason charged, "and that's the reason you're sitting up here waiting for Julia to come back. You've had that gas radiator going ever since before midnight. You haven't been to bed. Come on now, tell me the truth and tell it fast. We haven't got all day."

Her eyes faltered away from his. She twisted her fingers nervously. At that moment Mason heard the sound of rapid steps in the corridor. He stepped swiftly to the left of the door, standing where he would be concealed for the moment from anyone entering the room.

The doorknob turned. The door opened, then closed. Julia Branner, wearing a white rain coat which stretched almost to her ankles, her shoes soggy with water, her hair, as it showed beneath her hat, stringy and wet, clinging to the back of her neck, the curl completely removed, said in a high-pitched, almost hysterical voice, "Christ, Stella, I've got to get out of here! I'm in an awful jam. Let's get my things together, and you can drive me to the airport. I'm going back to Salt Lake. The most awful thing happened, I . . ." She broke off at what she saw in the other woman's eyes and whirled to stare at Perry Mason. *"You!"* she exclaimed.

Mason nodded and said calmly, "Suppose you sit down, Julia, and tell me just what did happen. It may help a lot if I know."

"Nothing happened."

Mason said, "Sit down, Julia, I want to talk with you."

"Listen, I'm in a hurry. I haven't any time to waste talking to you. It's too late for *you* to do any good now."

"Why is it too late?"

"Never mind."

She tossed her handbag on the table, fumbled with the buttons at the neck of her rain coat. Mason stepped forward, picked up her handbag, weighed it judiciously and said, "What happened to the gun you were carrying?"

Her face showed surprise. "Why, isn't it in there?"

"Listen," Mason told her, "if you want to waste time playing guessing games with me, that's your funeral, but Renwold Brownley was shot tonight by some woman wearing a white rain coat and driving a Chevrolet automobile. I think the police have a pretty good description of the automobile. Now, do you want me to try and help you, or do you want to play wise?"

Julia Branner stared at him speculatively, but Stella Kenwood gave a low moan and said, "Oh, Julia! I knew you'd do it!" and began to sob softly.

Mason met the hard-eyed defiance of Julia Branner's eyes and said, "Speak up."

"Why should I talk to *you*?" she asked, her voice bitter.

"I can help you," Mason told her.

"You could have helped me," she said, "but you didn't do a very good job of it and now it's too late."

"Why is it too late?"

"You know—but I don't know how you know."

Mason's voice showed his impatience. "Now listen, you two, seconds are precious and you're yapping around here like a couple of boobs. Snap out of it and get down to brass tacks. I'm going to help you, Julia."

"Why?" she asked. "I've got no money, not more than one hundred and fifty dollars altogether."

Stella Kenwood half rose from her chair and said hopefully, "I've got two hundred. You can have that, Julia."

"Let's forget about the money right now," Mason said. "I'm going to help you, Julia, but I *must* know what happened. I figure there's a lot to be said on your side of this thing no matter what you did. Brownley was absolutely cold and utterly remorseless. He'd framed a charge of manslaughter on you and held it over your head for years. He'd broken up any chance for domestic happiness you might have had and wouldn't give you even a thin dime. You had to work your way through life and there's a hell of a lot to be said on your side of this thing, but I want to know how bad it is. I won't guarantee that I'm going to stay with you all the way, but I'm going to start. Now go ahead and give me the lowdown. *Did* you kill Brownley?"

"No."

"Who did?"

"I don't know."

"You saw him tonight?"

"Yes."

"Where?"

"Down near the waterfront."

"Tell me what happened."

She shook her head and, in a voice which sounded suddenly flat and weary, said, "What's the difference? You wouldn't believe me. No one will believe me. Cut out the sobbing, Stella. I'm going to beat it. It's *my* funeral. You're not mixed up in it."

Mason said irritably, "Snap out of it! Tell me what happened. If anyone can help you, I can."

Julia Branner said, "Well, if you've got to know, I tried to bring some pressure to bear on Brownley."

"What pressure?"

"There was a watch he'd given Oscar when Oscar graduated from high school. The case was a family heirloom. Renwold had had new works put in it. He thought the world of it. I had the watch. I was carrying it the day Oscar skipped out to go back to his father. The old man wanted that watch about as much as he wanted anything on earth. I sent him a message by a cab driver and told him I wanted to talk with him for ten minutes, that if he'd come alone and at once to a certain place down at the beach and let me talk to him for ten minutes without interrupting me, I'd give him the watch."

"You thought he'd come?"

"I knew he'd come."

"You didn't think he'd have you arrested?"

"No. I told him the watch would be hidden, that the only way he could get it would be by playing square with me."

"So what?" Mason asked.

"He came."

"How did he know the place?"

"I drew him a little sketch map and told him where I'd meet him. I told him he'd have to come alone."

"Then what did you do?"

"Drove down to the harbor so I'd be there to meet him."

"What were you going to talk to him about?"

"I was going to make the only argument he'd ever have listened to. I was going to prove to him that my daughter had been the dead image of her father, that if he cared anything at all for Oscar he'd see that Oscar's flesh and blood didn't want for the good things of life. I was going to tell him that I didn't care what he did to me, with me or for me, that all I wanted was a square deal for Oscar's child. I was going to tell him that the girl who was pretending to be Oscar's child was an impostor."

"Why did you make him go all the way down to the water-front?"

"Because I wanted to."

"*Why* the water-front?"

"That's got nothing to do with it."

"Was your gun a .32 caliber Colt automatic?"

"Yes."

"What became of it?"

"I don't know. I missed it early this evening."

"Don't pull an old gag like that. It won't get you any place."

"It's the truth."

"And if you didn't kill Renwold Brownley, who did?"

"I don't know."

"Just what do you know?"

"I met him down by one of the yacht clubs," she said. "I told him to drive around a couple of the side streets to make certain he wasn't followed, then to come back to me. He drove around, came back and slowed down. He was about half a block away from me when some woman wearing a yellow rain coat made like mine ran out toward the car. Naturally, Brownley stopped. She jumped on the running board, and started to shoot."

"What did you do?"

"I turned and ran just as hard as I could."

"Where did you run to?"

"My car was parked about a block away."

"You jumped in it and drove away?"

"I had some trouble getting it started. It had been raining and the engine didn't go immediately."

"Did anyone see you?"

"I don't know."

"Where did you get the automobile?"

"It was Stella's car. I borrowed it."

"And that's the best story you can tell?"

"It's the truth."

Mason said slowly, "It may or may not be the truth. Personally, I don't think it is. One thing is certain: No jury would ever believe it. If you tell a story like that, you'll be stuck for first degree murder just as sure as you're sitting here. Pull down that bed, turn off that damned gas heater, open the windows, ditch that rain coat, undress and get into bed. If the police call for you, don't say a word. Don't make a single statement, no matter *what* they ask. Simply tell them you're not going to answer any questions unless your lawyer tells you to, and tell them I'm your lawyer."

She stared at him. "You mean you're going to stand by me and help me?"

"For a while, yes," he said. "Go on now, get your clothes

off and get into bed. And you, Stella, don't you say a word. Simply sit tight and keep quiet. Do you think you can do that?"

Stella Kenwood looked up with pale, frightened eyes and said, "I don't know. I don't think so."

"I don't either," Mason told her, "but do the best you can. Stall things along as long as you can in any event, and remember, Julia, don't *you* say a word, not to anyone. Don't answer questions and don't make any statements."

"You don't need to worry about me," she told him. "That's one of the things I'm good at."

Mason nodded, jerked the door open, stepped out into the corridor and, as he closed the door, heard the creak of springs as Julia Branner, calmly competent, pulled the wall bed into position.

Mason noticed that the rain had slackened to a cold drizzle. There was enough daylight to show low-flung clouds raising up from the southeast. The smell of a cold, wet dawn was in the air. He had just started the motor on his car when a police machine swung around the corner and slid to a stop in front of the Sunset Arms Apartments.

Chapter 9

Della Street was in the office when Perry Mason arrived the next morning. "And what's new?" he asked, tossing his hat on the top of the desk and grinning at the pile of mail.

"I presume you knew," she said, "that Julia Branner was arrested for the murder of Renwold Brownley?"

Mason widened his eyes in a look of simulated surprise and said, "No, I hadn't heard of it."

"The newspapers got out extras," she remarked. "Julia Branner says you're going to defend her, so you *should* know about it."

"No," Mason said, "this is a great surprise to me."

Della Street leveled a rigid forefinger at him, after the manner of a cross-examining attorney, and said, "Chief, where were you about daylight this morning?"

He grinned and said, "I can't tell a lie. I beat it from the Beechwood address about sixty seconds before the cops got there."

She sighed and said, "Some day you're not going to be so fortunate."

"It wouldn't have hurt," he said, "if they'd caught me there. I certainly had a right to interview my client."

"The newspaper also says that Julia Branner refuses to make any statement, but that a Stella Kenwood, who shared the apartment, while at first refusing to answer questions, has finally made a complete statement."

"Yes," Mason said, "she would."

The secretary's voice held a note of concern. "Can she tell them anything which would implicate you, Chief?"

"I don't think so," he said. "I don't think she can implicate anybody. What else is new?"

"Paul Drake wants to see you, says he has some news for

you. The wireless you sent to Bishop Mallory aboard the *Monterey* was not delivered because the *Monterey* has no William Mallory aboard." Mason gave a low whistle of surprise. Della Street consulted her notebook and said, "So I took the responsibility of sending a radiogram addressed to the Captain of the Steamship *Monterey* asking if Bishop William Mallory had sailed from Sydney on the northbound voyage and if so to ascertain definitely whether that same person was now aboard the ship either under that or some other name, first or second class."

Mason said, "Good girl. I'll have to think that over a bit. In the meantime, get Paul Drake on the line and tell him I want him to come in and bring Harry with him. What else is new, anything?"

"C. Woodward Warren wants an appointment with you. He talked with me and said he'd pay up to a hundred thousand dollars if you could save his son's life." Mason shook his head. "That's a lot of money," Della Street remarked.

"I know it's a lot of money," Mason said bitterly, "and I'm going to turn it down. That kid's nothing but the spoiled, pampered child of a millionaire. He's dished it out all of his life and never learned to take it. So when he ran up against the first real setback he'd ever had, he grabbed a gun and started shooting. Now he says he's sorry, and thinks everything should be smoothed out for him."

"You," Della Street said, "could get him off with a life sentence. That's all Mr. Warren can hope for. You'll defend this Branner woman and may not get a cent out of it, yet you're turning down a fee that's almost a fortune."

Mason said, "This Branner case has an element of mystery, a hint of poetic justice. There are all of the elements of a gripping human drama. I'm not definitely committing myself to go all the way in it. I'm going to use such talents as I may possess to see that justice is done. But, if I took that Warren case, I'd be using my talents and education to justify the sordid crime of the spoiled, pampered son of a foolish and indulgent father. Don't forget, this isn't the first scrape the kid's been in. He killed a woman with his car last year. The old man hushed it up and bought the kid free. Now he wants to bribe some lawyer to find some method by which the boy can cheat the gallows. To hell with 'em both! Get Paul Drake on the line and tell him to come in."

While she was putting through the call, Mason paced the floor, thumbs hooked in the armholes of his vest, head sunk forward in thought. He frowned at Della Street after a few seconds and said, "Shucks, Della, it's just down the corridor. You could run down there quicker than you could put through that call. What's the trouble?"

"The switchboard operator," she said, "was just giving me a wireless message which had been received from the *Monterey*. Just a moment and I'll read it." She said into the transmitter, "Get the Drake Detective Agency and tell Mr. Drake the Chief is waiting for him." Then she hung up the telephone and translated her shorthand: "BISHOP WILLIAM MALLORY WAS PASSENGER NORTHBOUND TRIP FROM SYDNEY SAT AT MY TABLE IS ABOUT FIFTY-FIVE IS FIVE FEET SIX OR SEVEN WEIGHT HUNDRED SEVENTY-FIVE OR EIGHTY IS DEFINITELY NOT ON SHIP NOW HAVE CHECKED ALL PASSENGERS. The message is signed CAPTAIN E. R. JOHANSON."

Mason nodded and said, "And I'll bet he did, too. He evidently realized it was something important."

"Perhaps the bishop stowed away somewhere," Della Street suggested.

Mason shook his head and said, "No, I'm betting on Captain Johanson. When he says a man is not aboard his ship, he means it."

"Then Drake must have been mistaken in thinking they saw him board the *Monterey* and not get off."

Mason said, "If he'd had suitcases with him, he could have . . ." His voice trailed away in silence. He stood staring thoughtfully at Della Street and said, "Send another message to Captain Johanson. Ask him if he can tell us if there are any suitcases aboard or in the baggage room with Bishop Mallory's name on the labels."

"You mean that he might have carried aboard a disguise?" she asked dubiously, "and then left the ship . . . ?"

"He went aboard in a disguise," Mason interrupted, laughing.

"What do you mean?"

"According to all accounts," Mason said, "his head was pretty much bandaged up. Now, I saw the room in the hotel right after he had been taken out in the ambulance. The counterpane was on the bed and there was an indentation in it where he'd been lying, but there wasn't any trace of blood. The man was evidently hit with a blackjack—something which usually bruises but doesn't break the skin. Now then, *why* should the bishop have wrapped his head in bandages which all but concealed his features?"

She stared at him with a puzzled frown and said, "But, Chief, Drake's men already knew what he looked like. It wouldn't have done any good to have concealed his features from them."

Mason grinned. "Have you ever gone down to the sailing of one of those big ships, Della?"

"No. Why?"

"Along at the last," he said, "there's a rush which jams the gangplank with a solid mass of jostling, pushing humanity. It's just a steady stream of faces marching past. Now if *you* were a detective and had seen a man go aboard in a black suit, with his head swathed in bandages, your mind would get just lazy enough to play tricks on you when the big rush started. In other words, you wouldn't study each face. You would subconsciously be looking for a bandaged head and a black suit. If your man walked down the gangplank wearing a tweed suit or an inconspicuous gray suit, with a felt hat pulled rather low on an unbandaged forehead, you'd unconsciously pass him up. Remember, things happen fast, and hundreds of people are funneled out of that gangplank, to disperse into a yelling mass of enthusiastic humanity."

Della Street nodded slow acquiescence and said, "Yes, I can see how something like that *could* have taken place. But . . ." She was interrupted by Paul Drake's code knock on Mason's private office.

Della Street opened the door. Paul Drake nodded to her and said in the thick accents of one who has a cold in his head, "Morning, Della. Come on in, Harry."

He and Harry Coulter entered the office, and Drake said

accusingly to the lawyer, "I let you talk me out of that last drink of whiskey last night, Perry, and look what happened to me."

Mason surveyed the watering eyes, the red nose, grinned unsympathetically and said, "You took too much on that first drink, Paul. It gave you a reaction too soon. How about you, Harry, how do *you* feel?"

"Swell," Coulter said, "and I was splashing around for hours before the Chief got there."

Drake slid into the big leather chair, swung his feet up over the overstuffed arm and shook his head sadly at Della Street. "That's what comes of trying to give service," he said. "Work yourself sick for a lawyer and you don't get any sympathy. It's a dog's life. A detective works day and night for a measly *per diem* while lawyers charge fees based on the results the detectives get for him."

Mason grinned and said, "That's the worst of a cold—it gives a man such a pessimistic outlook. Think how fortunate you are to have so much business, Paul. But if it's sympathy you're looking for, Della can hold your hand while you tell us what happened."

Drake suddenly galvanized into motion, his face twisting into contortions as his right hand shot for a hip pocket. He jerked out a handkerchief but failed to get it to his nose before he had sneezed explosively. He sadly wiped his nose, and said thickly, "The Seaton woman's disappeared. She didn't show at her apartment all night. I burgled the place again this morning and took a look around. It's just the way it was the last time we saw it."

Mason frowned thoughtfully. "She couldn't be hiding some place in the building, could she, Paul—perhaps in a friend's apartment?"

"I don't think so. Her toothbrush and tooth paste were hanging in a rack by the washbowl. She couldn't have gone out to get a new toothbrush and she'd almost certainly have sneaked back to the apartment to pick up hers even if she'd forgotten it when she went out to her friend's apartment."

"Then where is she?"

Drake shrugged his shoulders, twisted his face into a

grimace, and held his handkerchief beneath his nose. He held the pose for several seconds, then his features relaxed while he sighed and said, "That's another complaint I have against the whole scheme of existence. Every time I hold my handkerchief to my nose I can't sneeze. When I put it back in my pocket, I can't ever get it out in time. . . . Here's something funny, Perry: There are two other shadows on the job."

"Where?"

"Covering the Seaton house."

"Police?"

"No, I don't think so. My men figure them for private dicks."

"How do you know it's the Seaton girl they're after?"

"I don't, but it looks like it. One of them went up snooping around on the third floor. He may have even gone into the apartment. . . . What did you want with Harry?"

Mason turned to Harry Coulter. "Did Brownley go directly to the beach last night?" he asked.

"Yeah."

"And you were tagging along behind?"

"Uh huh."

"Did any other cars pass you?"

Coulter thought for a minute, and then said, "Yeah. There was a big yellow coupe went past just before we got to the beach, and it was going like hell. There may have been some other cars that passed me before that, but I don't remember them. I had my hands full tagging old Brownley through the rain. But this yellow coupe was making knots per hour, and it was after we'd passed the main drag that it went past us."

"In other words, you were pretty well down to the beach?"

"That's right."

"How many people in the car, one or two?"

"One I think. And I think the car was a Cadillac, but I can't be positive."

Mason said slowly, "Check up on the cars out at Brownley's place, Paul. See if anyone has a car that answers this description. Also, while you're about it, see if you can find out from the servants if there was any unusual activity around the house after Brownley left and . . ."

"Say, wait a minute," Harry interrupted, his forehead creased in a frown, "maybe I know more than I thought I did." Mason raised inquiring eyebrows. "Down by the yacht club," Coulter said, "there were some cars parked. They looked as though they'd been there for ages. You know the way those birds do when they are out on a cruise. They run their cars off to the side of the road in that parking place, lock them up and leave them. There are some garages down there but most of the fellows . . ."

"Yes, I know," Mason interrupted, "what about it?"

"Well," Coulter said, "when I was running around trying to pick up Brownley's trail down by the place where he keeps the yacht, there were four or five cars parked out in the rain. I was pretty sore at myself for letting Brownley get away from me and I looked 'em over—not with the idea of remembering the cars—just to see if Brownley's car was one of them. When I saw it wasn't, I kept on going. But, come to think of it, one of those cars was a big yellow coupe, a Cadillac, I think. Now that *may* have been the car that passed me. I couldn't have told, of course, because it was raining cats and dogs when the car went past. I saw headlights in my rear-view mirror, then there was a big wave of water, and a car went past with a rush. Then all I could see was a tail light—you know how it is when a car passes you on a rainy night."

As Mason nodded, Paul Drake sneezed again into his handkerchief and said, "That's the first sneeze I've timed right since I caught this damn cold."

"You couldn't have caught the cold down there this morning," Mason pointed out. "It wouldn't have developed that soon."

"Yeah, I know," Drake said. "Probably I haven't got any cold. You're like the guys who stroll around the decks of steamers, smoking pipes and telling the green-faced passengers there ain't any such thing as seasickness—that it's all in the imagination. Ordinarily I'd hate to do this to you, Perry, but since you've been so damned unsympathetic, it's going to be a pleasure. You can play around with all the yellow coupes you want to, but when you get done, you'll find you're no place.

This is one case where the police have got your client sewed up tight, and if you ain't careful they'll have you sewed up, too."

"What do you mean?" Mason asked.

"Just what I say. The police haven't been entirely asleep at the switch, and you left something of a back-trail yourself. The police can prove Brownley told you he was going to make a will which would put your client on the skids. They can trace you to a Western Union office where you sent a wireless to the *Monterey* and used a pay station telephone. They can prove you called Stella Kenwood's apartment where Julia Branner was staying.

"Now, *after* you telephoned Julia, she got a cab driver to take a letter to old man Brownley. Brownley read the letter and made some crack about having to go to the beach to get Oscar's watch back. He was excited as the devil."

"Did the cab driver give the letter to Brownley?" Mason asked.

"Not to the old man. He gave it to the grandson, and the grandson took it up. Old Brownley was asleep."

"Philip saw him read the letter?"

"That's right, and he said something to Philip about getting a watch back from Julia. Now the police figure she lured him down to the beach, climbed on the running board and gave him the works with a .32 automatic. She dropped the gun and beat it. An accomplice who was in on the play climbed into the car and drove it down to a pier, near which he had another car parked. He put the car in low gear, stood on the running board, opened the throttle, and jumped off. The car went into the drink."

"And I believe the car was still in low gear when they pulled it up, wasn't it?" Mason asked.

Drake, wiping his nose with his handkerchief, gave a muffled "Uh huh."

"And it's her gun," Coulter said. "She was carrying it under a permit issued in Salt Lake City."

Drake, sniffling, said, "What's more, they've got her finger-print on the car window on the left-hand side. You see, Brownley was driving with the window rolled up because it was raining. When Julia came out, he rolled the window down

96

to talk to her, but he didn't roll it all the way down. She stood on the running board, and hooked her fingers over the window and left some perfectly swell fingerprints on the inside of the glass. The cops got the car raised up before the water had eliminated the fingerprints."

Mason frowned. "Any chance she could have left her fingerprints on the car *before* Brownley started for the beach?"

"Not one chance in ten million," Drake said. "Now that's the gloomy side, Perry. Here's a silver lining to the cloud: There's a darn good chance this granddaughter who's living with Brownley *is* a phoney."

"Have you got any *facts*?" Mason asked.

"Of course I've got facts," Drake said irritably. "I don't know what they amount to, but they're facts. After Oscar's death the old man wanted to locate his granddaughter, so he got Jaxon Eaves to find her—or it may have been that Eaves came to old man Brownley and claimed that he could find the girl. I can't find out which is which.

"Now it isn't ethical for me to knock another detective agency, and it isn't nice to say anything against a man who's dead, but the story goes that old man Brownley agreed to pay twenty-five thousand dollars if Eaves could find the granddaughter. Now you figure twenty-five thousand bucks and add to it the possibility of a split on whatever inheritance the girl might get, and subtract that from Eaves' code of professional ethics, and you don't need to turn to the back of the book to find the answer. I will say this much for Eaves. He apparently tried his darnedest to locate the real granddaughter. He got as far as Australia, and then ran up against a brick wall.

"Now Eaves had a twenty-five thousand dollar bonus at stake, and that's a hell of a lot of money for a detective to pass up simply because he can't produce a granddaughter. And remember that about the only way you can prove an impostor ain't the real thing is to produce the real thing. Eaves had gone far enough with his investigation to become pretty well satisfied the real thing couldn't be produced. Now, of course, the old man wanted proof before he paid over the money, but he also *wanted* to believe the girl was genuine. He wanted to be convinced. Eaves and the girl wanted to convince him. There wasn't anyone to take the other end of the argument. That's something like having a lawyer argue his case to the judge without having any witnesses or any lawyer on the other side."

Mason said thoughtfully, "You figure Eaves arranged with the girl to split any inheritance she'd get?"

Drake said impatiently, "Of course he did. Don't think Eaves would overlook a bet like that."

"And he's dead?"

"Uh huh."

Mason said slowly, "He wouldn't have kept this all to himself, Paul. There must have been someone else in on the deal, and now that Eaves is dead, there must be someone trailing along to get Eaves' cut out of the inheritance."

Drake nodded his head and said, "That's logical, but I can't prove anything."

"And then again someone who smells a rat might be trying to cut in, just on general principals," Mason pointed out.

"That's not so likely," Drake said. "It's a good set-up for a blackmailer, *if* the blackmailer knew what he was doing; but old Brownley wasn't a damned fool, and neither was Jaxon Eaves. They didn't make any splash in the newspapers when the girl moved in. She just slid quietly into the house and started living there, and Brownley casually announced she was his granddaughter, and after a while, the society editors started telling every time she went to Palm Springs and what she had on."

Mason nodded his head slowly. "Is she staying at the house now, Paul?" he asked.

"No, she left the place early this morning and went to the Santa Del Rios Hotel. You know a young kid like that didn't want to be around the house after the tragedy."

"That's what she says?" Mason asked.

"That's what she says," Paul Drake affirmed.

"Of course," Mason said, "she might have gone to the hotel so she could be more available for conferences with anyone who was interested in keeping her out of the murder mix-up."

Drake sneezed, wiped his nose and said, "I'm keeping her shadowed."

Mason started pacing the floor, his forehead puckered into a frown. Once or twice he shook his head dubiously, then paused in his pacing to stand with feet spread far apart and stare moodily at the detective. "That isn't going to get us anywhere, Paul," he said. "That's the sort of net which will catch all the small fish but let all the big ones get away."

"What do you mean?" Drake asked.

"If she's there in the hotel and some man is planning her campaign, that man will either be a detective or will be someone who was associated with Eaves when Eaves was alive. In other words, he'll know all about how detectives work and what to watch out for. He'll know darn well that we're having the girl shadowed, and he'll have some scheme figured out by which that shadowing won't do us any good, at least so far as he's concerned."

"Well," Drake said irritably, "what the hell can *I* do?"

Mason said slowly, "Nothing. We can't get in touch with the man we want by trying to follow his *back* trail." He turned to Della Street and said, "Della, could you get a henna pack that would make your hair look nice and red?"

"Yes. Why?"

Mason said moodily, "You could go into the Seaton girl's apartment just as though you owned the joint, finish packing up, take her trunk and suitcase and go to some new apartment."

"Wouldn't that put her in an awful spot?" Drake asked.

Mason, speaking in the moody monotone of one who is thinking out loud, said, "Breaking and entry, grand larceny and a few other things—*if* they could prove a criminal intent. If they *couldn't* prove criminal intent, there wouldn't be so much to it."

"But what would be the advantage?" Drake inquired.

"If the chaps who are watching that house," Mason said slowly, "are hired by someone who's interested in getting Eaves' cut out of the estate, they won't know anything about Janice Seaton except what they've been able to pick up from a description, and that'll mostly be a trim figure with red hair. When they see someone who answers that description checking out of the Seaton girl's apartment, they'll act on the assumption that two and two make four and won't ask her to go down to the bank to be identified."

Harry Coulter fidgeted uneasily in his chair and said, "You can't tell just what they're after, Mason. Looking at it one way . . ." He became silent in mid-sentence and shrugged his shoulders.

Della Street went to the closet, took out her hat and coat. "It'll take me about two hours to get that pack and get my hair dry, Chief," she said.

Mason nodded. The other two men stared at her in apprehensive silence.

Chapter 10

Mason waited in front of the hotel apartment house and frowningly consulted his wristwatch. He lit a cigarette and nervously paced up and down a strip of pavement. When the cigarette was half finished, a taxicab swung around the corner, with a small wardrobe trunk held in place by a strap. Mason gave one quick look at the cab, flipped his cigarette into the gutter, stepped back into the entrance of the apartment hotel and waited until he saw Della Street, her hair a bright auburn, step from the cab.

Mason turned, entered the lobby, nodded reassuringly to the clerk on duty at the desk and said, "I have my key, thanks." He rode up in the elevator to the tenth floor and opened the door of 1028. He closed the door, dragged up a chair, climbed on it and stood where he could look over the transom at 1027, which was directly across the corridor.

A few minutes later, he heard the sound of an elevator door, quick steps in the corridor, and then the rumble of wheels made by a hand truck. Della Street, preceded by one of the porters who carried a suitcase in one hand, a bag in the other, walked down the corridor. The porter paused in front of Room 1027 and said, "This is it—the one you reserved over the telephone. If it isn't right, we can change it."

"I'm quite sure it will be all right," Della Street said. "I'm familiar with the apartments. I had a friend who lived here once."

The porter opened the door, stood aside for Della to enter, then followed her with the suitcase. A second or two later, an assistant trundled the trunk into the apartment.

Mason leaned his arm against the sill of the transom and eased his weight against the wood. He saw the porter and the assistant come out to the corridor with broad smiles on their faces, closing the door behind them.

There followed a long, tedious wait, while Mason shifted his position and smoked cigarettes, the stubs of which he ground out against the wood of the transom. He stiffened to attention as he heard the clang of the elevator door and then steps in the corridor. A tall man walked swiftly down the carpeted hallway. There was something furtive in his manner, despite the fact that he made no attempt to tread lightly. The man paused in front of Mason's door, raised his knuckles as though to knock, then squinted his eyes as he stared up at the number, turned sharply about, and knocked on the door of apartment 1027.

Della Street's voice called, "Who is it?"

"The engineer to inspect your light connections," the man said.

Della Street opened the door. The man entered the room without a word. The door shut with some violence.

Mason finished his cigarette and looked at his wristwatch. Seconds ticked into minutes. After five minutes, Mason started to smoke another cigarette, but extinguished it after taking no more than two puffs. From across the hall came the sound of a faint thud, a mere hint of muffled noise. Mason jumped down to the floor, sent the chair spinning half across the room with a quick twist of his wrist, jerked the door open, crossed the corridor in three swift strides, and twisted the knob of the door of 1027. The door was locked.

Mason, moving with cat-like agility, stepped back, lowered his shoulder, and went forward in a charge. He flung his full weight against the locked door, like a football player with only seconds to play in the final quarter bucking the line. Wood splinted as the lock gave way. The door slammed back on its hinges, struck against a door-stop, and came to a shivering pause. Mason saw a pair of wildly kicking legs, the broad shoulders of a man bending over a slender, struggling figure. Bedclothes had been dragged out from beneath the studio couch on which the pair were struggling, and the tall man was holding a thick quilt down on Della Street's face, muffling her cries, slowly suffocating her. He jumped to his feet and whirled to face Mason, his mouth distorted with the intensity of his

102

effort, as a sprinter's face is twisted into a spasm when nearing the tape. The man's hand raced back to his hip pocket. "Hold it," he warned. Mason came forward in a charge.

Della Street flung off the quilt. The tall man whipped blued steel from his pocket. Mason, some ten feet away, stared into the ominous dark hole which marked the end of a .38 caliber revolver. The man braced his shoulder as though against an expected recoil. His lips were twisted back from his teeth. Mason stopped abruptly, shifted his eyes to Della Street. "Are you hurt, kid?" he asked.

"Get your hands up," the man with the gun warned. "Back up against that wall. When you get there, turn to face it and hold your hands just as high as . . ."

Della Street doubled up her body, braced her heels and shot forward. The man jumped to one side, but not in time to keep her from grabbing the arm which held the gun. Mason took two jumps and swung his right fist, catching the man flush on the jaw. The tall man staggered backward. Della Street, clutching for the gun, slid down the man's arm and fell, face forward, on the floor. She jerked the weapon from the man's nerveless fingers. The tall man regained his balance, lashed out a vicious kick at Mason, and picked up a chair.

Della Street, rolling over, the gun in her hand, screamed, "Watch out for him, Chief! He's a killer!"

Mason feinted a rush, stopped abruptly.

The man whirled the chair in a vicious swing, tried to check the momentum of that swing when he realized Mason's rush was a feint, but spun half around, off balance. He dropped the chair, and grabbed for Mason as the lawyer rushed. Mason knocked the man's left aside and sent his fist crashing into the other's nose. He felt the cartilage flatten out under the impact of his fist, saw the man stagger backward and drop abruptly to his hips. The tall man tried to say something, but the words only bubbled through the red smear which had been his nose and lips.

Della Street climbed to her feet, Mason caught the man by the collar, jerked him upright, spun him around, and slammed him down on the couch where he had been struggling with Della. The lawyer's hands made a swiftly thorough job of searching the man for weapons. "All right, buddy," he said, "talk!"

The man made gurgling sounds, pulled a handkerchief from his coat pocket, carried it to his mutilated face, and lowered it, a sodden, red rag.

Della Street ran from the bathroom with towels. Mason handed the man one of the towels and said to Della, "Get some cold water." She brought in a pan of cold water. Mason sopped one of the towels in the water, held it against the back of the man's neck, dashed cold water over his face. The man said, in a thick, choking voice, the words sounding as though someone was holding a clothespin over his nose, "You've broken my nose."

"What the hell did you think I was trying to do," Mason asked, "kiss you? You're damned lucky I didn't break your neck!"

"I'll have you arrested for this," the man choked out.

Mason told him, "You'd find yourself facing a charge of assault with intent to commit murder. What did he do, Della?"

Della Street was half hysterical. "He got rough, Chief," she said, "and when I tried to blow the whistle to signal you, he jumped on me, punched the wind out of me, jerked the bedclothes out of the closet and tried to smother me. He was going to kill me."

The man groaned as he held towels to his face.

Mason said savagely, "I should have beaten your head in with a club; but, damn it, now I've spoiled your looks so Bishop Mallory can't identify you as the man who knocked him over the head."

Unintelligible words sounded thickly from behind the soggy towels.

Mason said, "Hell, we're not getting anywhere doing this. Let's see who this bird is." He calmly proceeded to go through the man's pockets. The man tried to push Mason away, then clutched his fingers for Mason's throat. Mason said, "Not enough yet, eh?" and jabbed his fist into the pit of the other's stomach. As the struggle ceased he pulled objects from the man's pockets and handed them to Della Street. He discovered and passed over a wallet, a key container, a knife, a watch, a

104

blackjack, a package of cigarettes, a cigarette lighter, fountain pen, pencil, and then a single key which had not been clipped into the leather key container. "Look 'em over, Della," he said, "and let's see who this bird is."

The man had fallen back on the couch now and lay perfectly motionless, only the hoarse sound of his sputtering breath, coming from behind the towels, showed that he was still alive. Della Street said, "He tried to murder me. I can tell the difference between someone just trying to smother my cries and someone really trying to kill me."

"All right," Mason said, "let's see who he is. Something tells me when we find out how this bird fits into the picture, we'll know a lot more than we do now."

Della laughed nervously as she opened the wallet. "My hand's shaking," she said. "Gosh, Chief, I was sc-c-ared."

Mason said, "We'll settle his hash. He's the one who knocked the bishop on the head. We can send him up for having that blackjack in his possession."

"Here's a driving license," she said, "made out to Peter Sacks. The address is 691 Ripley Building."

"Okay," Mason said, "what else?"

"Here are some business cards," she said, "State-Wide Detective Agency, Incorporated. Here's a license made out to Peter Sacks as a private detective."

Mason whistled.

"There are some papers in the wallet. Do you want those?"

"Everything."

"Here's a hundred dollars in twenties. Here's a wireless addressed to Bishop William Mallory, Steamship *Monterey*. It reads: CHARLES W. SEATON KILLED SIX MONTHS AGO IN AUTOMOBILE ACCIDENT. I AM SETTLING HIS ESTATE. WRITING YOU IMPORTANT LETTER CARE OF MATSON COMPANY, SAN FRANCISCO. [Signed] JASPER PELTON, ATTORNEY."

"Now we're getting some place," Mason said. "What else, Della?"

"Here's a letter," she said, "from Jasper Pelton, an attorney in Bridgeville, Idaho. It's addressed to Bishop William Mallory, passenger on Steamship *Monterey*, care of Matson Navigation Company, San Francisco."

105

"Go ahead and read it," Mason said.

"My dear Bishop [she read], as the attorney settling the estate of Charles W. Seaton, I have received the radiogram which you sent Mr. Seaton, asking him to communicate with you immediately upon your arrival in San Francisco.

"Mrs. Seaton died some two years ago, leaving surviving her Charles W. Seaton and a daughter, Janice. Some six months ago Mr. Seaton was fatally injured in an auto wreck. He died within twenty-four hours after the injuries were received. At his bedside at the time of his death was his daughter, Janice, who is a trained nurse. I am mentioning this to you in detail because, during a lucid interval just before his death, Mr. Seaton very apparently tried to give us some message to be conveyed to you. He said several times, 'Bishop Mallory. Tell him . . . promise . . . don't want . . . read in news-paper . . .'

"I am giving you this verbatim because I took down as many of the words as we could understand. Unfortunately, Seaton was too weak to articulate clearly and most of his words were merely a rattle which could not be understood. He apparently sensed this and made several desperate attempts to get his message across, but died without being able to do so.

"At the time, I searched diligently throughout the United States for a Bishop Mallory, thinking that perhaps he might be able to shed some light upon what Mr. Seaton had been trying to tell us. I located a Bishop Mallory in New York and one in Kentucky. Neither of them remembered a Mr. Seaton, although they stated it might well have been possible Mr. Seaton had been in touch with them and they had forgotten about him, inasmuch as bishops come in contact with so many people.

"Mr. Seaton at one time had been in the possession of considerable property, but his financial affairs had become hopelessly involved within the last two years and, after deducting the claims which have been presented and allowed from the inventory value of the estate, it is doubtful if there will be much property to turn over to the daughter who is now, I believe, somewhere in Los Angeles. I do not have her present address, but will endeavor to get in touch with her through friends of hers and ask her to communicate with you. If you happen to be in Los Angeles you might locate her through the fact that she is a registered nurse.

"I am giving you this detailed information because I was a personal friend of Mr. Seaton, as well as a member of a fraternal organization in which he was active. I would like very much indeed to be able to send Janice something substantial from the estate, and if you know of any tangible or potential assets I would be glad to have you communicate with Miss Janice Seaton or with me."

"That all of it?" Mason asked.

"That's all of it except the signature. It's an awful scrawl."

"Well," Mason said, "we're commencing to get somewhere. Those are the papers that he . . ." He broke off as a voice from the door said, "What's coming off here?"

Mason whirled to face a dignified elderly gentleman whose close-cropped white mustache contrasted with the rich red of a florid complexion. The eyes were cold, steely and steady. From all appearances, the man might have been a banker, but there was an ominous menace in his eyes.

Mason said, "Where do *you* fit into the picture?"

"I'm Victor Stockton," the man said. "Does that mean anything to you?"

"No," Mason told him.

"You don't mean anything to me either."

Sacks, on the couch, had struggled to a sitting position at the sound of Stockton's voice. He pulled the bloody towels from his face. The frosty, gray eyes shifted from Mason to Sacks. "What did he do to you, Pete?" Stockton asked.

Sacks tried to say something, but his swollen lips and broken nose made the words inaudible.

Stockton turned back to Mason. "This man's my partner," he said. "I'm working with him on this case. I don't know who you are, but I'm going to find out."

Mason, his hands at his side, said, "Your friend Mr. Sacks broke into Bishop Mallory's room in the Regal Hotel and stole some papers. Were you in partnership with him on *that* deal?"

Stockton's eyes remained cold, nor did they so much as falter, but a film seemed to have been drawn over them. "Got any proof?" he asked.

Mason said, "You're damned right I've got proof."

Sacks made a lunge and tried to grab the letter from Della Street's hand. Mason caught his shoulder and pushed him back. Stockton started forward, his hand clawing at his hip.

Mason felt Della Street's body pressed against him, felt his right arm pulled slightly back. She pushed the cold butt of the .38 Mason had knocked from the detective's hand into his fingers. Mason moved his right hand forward. Stockton glimpsed the gun and froze into immobility. Mason said to Della Street, "Take down that phone and ask for police headquarters. Tell them . . ."

The man with the battered face swung his feet to the floor. Stockton nodded his head. Sacks ran in a staggering rush past Stockton, out of the door and down the corridor. Stockton turned deliberately on his heel and walked slowly from the room, pulling the door shut behind him.

Mason said to Della Street, "Are you hurt, kid?"

She smiled at him, shook her head, and explored her throat with the tips of her fingers. "The big baboon," she said, "tried to choke me. Then he got a knee in my stomach and got the bedclothes over my head."

"Did he know you were trying to signal me?" Mason asked.

"I don't think so. I tried to blow the whistle when the party got rough. I tell you, Chief, he was desperate. I saw panic and murder in his eyes. He's frightened stiff at something, and he's like a cornered rat."

Mason nodded and said, "Of course he's frightened."

"At what?" she asked.

Mason said, "Janice Seaton is the real granddaughter of Renwold Brownley. These detectives were in on the original crooked substitution and they've *got* to make it stick. With Brownley dead, they'll get a cut from the fake granddaughter, which'll make them independently wealthy. They're gambling with a fortune on one side and jail on the other."

"Wouldn't it have been logical for them to have killed Brownley?"

"Lots of people could logically have killed him," Mason told her. "My job is to find who *did* kill him."

"What'll I do with this stuff?"

108

"Give it to me," Mason said.

"You're going to keep it?"

"I'll hold it for evidence."

"Won't it be larceny? There's money in that purse. He might file a complaint. . . ."

Mason interrupted savagely, "To hell with him! When the time comes, I'll turn these letters over to Jim Pauley, the house dick at the Regal, and he'll make a complaint charging these birds with burgling the bishop's room."

"You caved in the whole front of that man's face, Chief," she said.

His eyes were smoldering as he looked at her, his jaw pushed aggressively forward, "I wish to hell," he said, "that I'd made a better job of it." He crossed to the telephone, called Drake's agency, frowned when informed Drake was at a Turkish bath, and said to Drake's secretary, "Get all the dope you can on a private detective by the name of Peter Sacks. He thought Della Street was the Seaton girl and tried to bump her off. . . . Get your men busy on that angle." Mason hung up the telephone. "Okay, kid," he said, "you go back to the office."

"Where are you going?" she asked.

"I," he told her grimly, "am going to the Santa Del Rios Hotel to interview the spurious granddaughter of Renwold C. Brownley."

Chapter 11

Mason folded a twenty-dollar bill and slid it into the palm of the girl at the switchboard in the Santa Del Rios Hotel. "All I ask," he said, "is that you get her on the line for me. I'll take care of things after that."

"I have positive orders," she demurred. "She's been deluged by newspaper reporters."

"And she's dodging publicity?"

"I'll say. She's overcome with grief."

"Yeah," Mason said, "overcome with grief because she's inherited a few million and is going to get her paws on it."

"Are you a newspaper man?" the girl at the switchboard asked. Mason shook his head. "What then?"

"To you," Mason told her, "I'm Santa Claus."

She sighed and her fingers closed over the twenty dollars. "If I nod my head," she said, "get in booth two. I'll have her on the line. That's all I can do."

"That's all you have to do," Mason told her. "What's her number?"

"She's in Suite A on the second floor."

"Okay," Mason remarked and stepped back from the desk. The nimble fingers of the girl flew over the switchboard. From time to time she talked into the mouthpiece which was held in position on her chest so that the curved rubber transmitter was within a few inches of her lips. Suddenly she turned to Mason and nodded. Mason entered the booth, picked up the receiver and said, "Hello." A feminine voice of silken texture said, "Yes, what is it?"

Mason said, "I'm Mr. Mason here in the hotel, and I think I should discuss with you arrangements we're perfecting to keep newspaper reporters from bothering you. We've had a perfect swarm of them down here. They've been ordered to get interviews or else, and unless we cooperate I'm afraid you'll be seriously annoyed."

The voice said, "That'll be fine, Mr. Mason. I appreciate what you're doing."

"May I come up now?" Mason asked.

"Yes. Go to 209 and tap on the door. I'll let you in through there. Don't come to Suite A. I think that's being watched by the newspaper men."

Mason thanked her, hung up, took the elevator to the second floor and knocked on the door of 209. It was opened by an attractive young woman in green lounging pajamas who flashed him a seductive smile and locked the door behind him. Then she led the way through connecting doors across two bathrooms and three conventionally furnished hotel bedrooms, into a corner suite at the end of the wing, where luxurious furnishings and deep carpets created the atmosphere of a palatial home.

She nodded toward a chair and said, "How about a cigarette and a little Scotch and soda?"

"Thanks," said Mason.

While he selected a cigarette, she poured Scotch from a cut-glass decanter into a tall glass, dropped in ice cubes and squirted carbonated water into the glass. "Have you heard any news?" she asked. "Have they found Grandfather's body?"

"Not yet," he told her. "This must be quite a shock to you."

"It is," she said, "a terrible shock," and placed a jeweled hand to her eyes.

"Can you," Mason said, settling back in his chair, "remember anything of your early childhood?"

"Why of course," she told him, removing her hand and staring at him in steady appraisal.

"You were an adopted child, I believe."

"Say, what's the idea?" she asked, her eyes suddenly wary, her muscles stiffening as though she were ready to run. "You said you wanted to see me about keeping out newspaper reporters."

Mason nodded easily and said, "That was the stall Pete told

me to use to fool the telephone girl. I supposed he'd tipped you off on it."

"Pete?" she asked, raising her eyebrows.

"Sure," Mason said, blowing out a casual puff of cigarette smoke.

"I don't know what you're talking about."

Mason frowned impatiently. "Listen! I haven't got all day on this thing. Pete Sacks and Victor Stockton told me to get in touch with you. Pete said not to let you know who I was, because he was afraid someone might be listening in on the telephone calls, so I was to pull that stall about keeping the newspaper reporters away from you, and he was to tip you off what it meant so I wouldn't have any trouble getting in. When you told me to come on up, I figured of course Pete had been in touch with you."

Her eyes studied the pink polish on her fingernails for almost ten seconds before she said, "Who are you?"

Mason said, "Look here; there's no chance Pete's double-crossing both of us, is there? You came over on the *Monterey* with Bishop Mallory, didn't you?"

She nodded her head, started to say something, then changed her mind, hesitated a moment.

Mason heard the faint sound of a door-latch clicking behind him, but was afraid to turn his head.

"Just who *are* you?" the girl asked again, and this time her voice seemed filled with more confidence.

A man standing in the doorway said, "His name's Perry Mason. He's a lawyer representing a couple of blackmailers who are trying to shake down the estate for a nice piece of change."

Mason slowly turned and encountered the steely eyes of Victor Stockton.

"A lawyer!" Janice Brownley exclaimed, getting to her feet, her voice showing consternation.

"Yes. What have you told him?"

"Nothing."

Stockton nodded and said to Mason, "It's time you and I had a little talk."

Mason said grimly, "When I talk to you, it'll be on the witness stand and under oath."

Stockton moved easily across the room, dropped into a chair and said, "Pour me a drink, Janice." His watchful eyes didn't leave Mason's face.

Janice Brownley splashed Scotch into a glass and fumbled for ice cubes with the silver tongs. Stockton settled back in the chair comfortably and said to Mason, "Don't be too sure. There's a warrant out for your arrest."

"For *my* arrest!" Mason exclaimed.

Stockton nodded and grinned. "Grand larceny, assault with a deadly weapon, and robbery," he said.

Mason's shrewd eyes studied the other man in critical appraisal. "Because of Sacks?" he asked.

"Because of Sacks," Stockton said. "You can't pull that stuff and get away with it."

Mason remarked grimly, "The hell I can't. You haven't seen anything yet. I *was* going to let the matter drop. But if you want to go ahead with it, we'll see where you get off. Sacks tried to commit murder. He pulled a gun on me and I smashed his nose and took it away from him. He got off lucky."

Stockton said to Janice Brownley, "Not too much soda, Janice." He turned his frosty back to Mason and said, "Listen, I'm a detective. Pete's working for me. We've known for more than three weeks an attempt was going to be made to shake Brownley down. I didn't know just *how* it was going to be done. I figured it would be played through some lawyer. A smart lawyer would have kept himself in the clear by going to Brownley first and then letting Janice come to him with a proposition. A boob would have laid himself wide open to blackmail charges by coming to Janice first. In either event, it was a shakedown, so I figured on beating you to the punch. I tipped the old man off, and I told Janice just what she could expect. We were laying for you. Then you stole a march on us by killing the old man. . . . Now, keep your shirt on. I don't say *you* did it, but you know who did it and *I* know who did it. That's put us in a funny spot, particularly if there isn't any will, or if the will should leave property to the granddaughter without specifying that by the word granddaughter he means the girl who is living in his house with him."

Janice Brownley silently handed him the glass. Stockton clinked the ice against the sides of the glass and raised it to his lips.

"So what?" Mason asked.

Stockton said, "You'd like to have me tell you that if you'd step out of the case, Pete Sacks would drop the charges against you. Then you'd use that statement to show the D.A. we were trying to use him for a cat's-paw. Well, Mr. Perry Mason, you've got another guess coming. That's a trap I'm not walking into."

"I'm still listening," Mason told him.

Stockton said slowly, measuring his words with scrupulous care, "It might be better *business* for Janice to make some sort of compromise. It's going to be darned near impossible for her to prove her relationship. On the other hand, it's going to be utterly impossible for anyone to disprove it."

"You have something in mind?" Mason asked.

"Have you?" Stockton countered.

"No."

"No offer of settlement?"

"None whatever."

Stockton said, "All right then, we're going to fight every inch of the way. There'll be no compromise. You've seen fit to mix in this thing, and now you're going to take it right on the chin. If you'd stayed in your office, minding your own business and practicing law, you'd have been in the clear. You didn't do that. You went running around, playing detective and acting smart. Now you've bit into something, and I'm going to let you try and chew it. Julia Branner had a pipe-dream which didn't work, so she bumped Brownley off to keep him from making a will which would knock her scheme into a cocked hat. It might have been a swell break if Bixler hadn't seen the whole thing. The way it stands now, Julie Branner's going to be convicted of murder as a principal. The girl she's trying to palm off as her daughter is going to be convicted of being an accessory after the fact, and you're going to be disbarred and convicted of assault with a deadly weapon, grand larceny, and robbery. After that, you can figure how a jury will feel about giving you three birds a slice of the estate— And don't slam the door as you go out."

114

Mason said, "I'm not slamming any doors just yet. And, by the way, Janice, where were *you* when your grandfather was killed?"

Stockton set down his glass. His face darkened a shade. "So," he said, "you're going to try something like that, eh?"

"I just asked a question," Mason said.

"Well, you ask too damn many questions. And, in case you want to know, Janice has a perfect alibi. She was with me."

A slow smile spread over Mason's face and he said, "Well, now *isn't* that nice. Janice is a ringer you've planted on the old man. She's about to get shown up and you are desperate so you . . ."

"Steal Julia Branner's gun, forge her name to a letter, and bump off the old man," Stockton interrupted. "The weak part about that is the taxi driver knows it was Julia who sent the message which lured the old man down to the beach. It was Julia Branner's fingerprints the police found on the car where she'd hung onto the window while she emptied her gun into him. It was Julia Branner's gun that did the killing, and it was Julia Branner's wet clothes the police found in her apartment when they made the pinch, before she'd quite got in bed."

"And in addition," Janice Brownley said, "there were . . ."

"Keep out of this, Janice," Stockton interrupted, without shifting his eyes from the lawyer. "*I'll* do the talking."

"Yes," Mason said sarcastically, "he's your alibi, Janice. *He* swears you were with him when the murder was committed, so *you* couldn't have done it, and *you* swear he was with you, so *he* couldn't have done it."

Stockton grinned and said, "And don't forget my wife. She was there, and a notary public who lives across the hall that I'd called in to make an additional witness." Stockton finished the last of his drink. His grin was slow, deliberate and unfriendly. "I've told you enough so you can see what you're up against," he said, "and that's *all* you're going to find out from us."

"What do you want?" Mason asked.

"Nothing."

"What's your proposition?"

Stockton grinned and said, "We haven't any. And what's more, we aren't going to make any. You're going to be too much on the defensive from now on to rig up any more blackmailing schemes."

Mason said sarcastically, "I presume that after Pete Sacks broke into Bishop Mallory's room, sapped the bishop with a blackjack and stole the bishop's private papers, the D.A. will consider it a felony for someone who's representing Bishop Mallory to recover the papers?"

Stockton shook his head. "Don't be funny. You know why you framed Pete into that trap just as well as I do. You wanted the key."

There was genuine surprise in Mason's voice. "The key?" he asked.

Stockton nodded.

"What key?"

"The one you got," Stockton said grimly. "Don't play so damn innocent."

"I got a *bunch* of keys," Mason said.

"As well as a hundred dollars in cash and a few other things. But what you wanted was *the* key."

Mason kept his face without expression. Stockton studied him for a moment and said, "Don't act so damn innocent.— Hell, you may be just a sucker, at that. How the hell do you suppose we knew the inside of this blackmail racket? We had a line into Julia Brownley before she even came to California. She figured Pete was a torpedo who was willing to bump anyone off, and she played right into his hands. She put up a proposition to Pete to kill Brownley before he could make another will. She had a man who was going to pose as Bishop Mallory long enough to make a deposition which would identify Janice Seaton as the real granddaughter. This bishop was a phoney who had been carefully rehearsed in the part he was to play. She might have fooled the old man, or she might even have been able to get a shake-down from Janice here, if she hadn't spilled the whole dope to Pete. She was playing Pete to be her right-hand man. She was going to get some lawyer who could put up a good fight, sell him on her story, and let him contact Brownley. If Brownley was willing to kick through in order to avoid a stink, she'd settle. If Brownley got tough, she was going to bump him off, and Pete was the one she'd picked to do the dirty work. She gave Pete a key to her apartment and promised him twenty-five percent of whatever she and Janice Seaton got out of the deal. And, just to show you what a sucker you are, she'd even planned to contact the old man behind your back after you'd broken the ice. She was going to make a settlement with him and leave you out in the cold, and if she couldn't scare the old man into a settlement, she was going to try and shake the granddaughter down for a few thousand and leave you holding the sack.—At that she might have had us worried if we hadn't had Pete in on the ground floor.

"After the murder, you were mixed in so deep you had to get her out in order to get yourself out. You had to get that key from Pete, because that key corroborated his testimony. So you trapped Pete into an apartment where you could beat him up and grab the evidence, but we've got just a little more on Julia Branner than you figured. You've made your bed, and now you can die in it."

Mason got to his feet. Stockton set down the empty glass, took a step toward Mason and said, "And don't come here any more. Do you get that?"

Mason stared at the man moodily. "I have," he said, slowly, "already smashed one nose, and I'd just as soon smash another."

Stockton stood still, neither retreating nor advancing. "And you have already stolen some papers which were evidence in the case," he said. "When Pete tried to get back that evidence you swung on him and pulled a gun on me. Don't forget that. And *if* you keep on playing around with this bunch of blackmailers you're tied up with, you'll probably find yourself mixed in a murder charge."

Mason strode toward the door, but turned in the doorway. "How much of a cut are you supposed to get out of the inheritance for having dug up an heir to the estate?" he asked.

Stockton grinned mirthlessly and said, "Don't bother about

it now, Mason. Write me a letter from San Quentin. You'll have more time to think things over when you get up there."

Mason left the room, took the elevator to the lobby, and was halfway across the sidewalk when someone touched him on the arm. He whirled to encounter Philip Brownley. "Hello," he said, "what are *you* doing here?"

Brownley said grimly, "I'm keeping watch on Janice."

"Afraid something's going to happen to her?" Mason asked.

Brownley shook his head and said, "Look here, Mr. Mason, I want to talk with you."

"Go on and talk," Mason told him.

"Not here."

"Where?"

"My car's parked at the curb. I saw you go in, and called to you, but you didn't hear me. I was waiting for you to come out. Let's sit in my car and talk."

Mason said, "I don't like the climate around here. A man by the name of Stockton is playing smart. . . . Do you know Stockton?"

Brownley said slowly, "He's the one who helped Janice kill Grandfather."

Mason's eyes bored steadily into Brownley's. "Are you just talking?" he asked. "Or are you saying something?"

"I'm saying something."

"Where's your car?"

"Over here."

"All right. Let's get in it."

Brownley opened the door of a big gray cabriolet and slid in behind the steering wheel. Mason climbed in beside him, sitting next to the curb, and pulled the door shut.

"This your car?" he asked.

"Yes."

"All right, what about Janice?"

There were dark circles under Brownley's eyes. His face was white and haggard. He lit a cigarette with a hand that trembled, but when he spoke his voice was steady. "I took the message the cab driver left last night—or rather this morning," he said.

"What did you do with it?"

118

"Took it up to my grandfather."

"Was he asleep?"

"No. He'd gone to bed, but he wasn't sleeping. He was reading a book."

"So what?" Mason asked.

"He read the message and got excited as the devil. He jumped into his clothes and told me to have someone get his car out, that he was going down to the beach to meet Julia Branner; that Julia had promised to give him back Oscar's watch if he'd come alone without being followed and go aboard his yacht where she could talk with him without being interrupted."

"He told you that?" Mason asked.

"Yes."

"What did you do?"

"I advised him not to go."

"Why?"

"I thought it was a trap."

Mason's eyes narrowed slowly. "Did you think someone would try to kill him?"

"No. Of course not. But I thought they might try to trap him into some compromising situation, or into making statements."

Mason nodded. There was a moment or two of silence, and then the lawyer said. "Go on. This is your party. You're doing the talking."

"I went down personally and opened the garage so Grandfather could get his car out. When he came down I begged him to let me drive him. It was a mean night, and Grandfather isn't . . . wasn't . . . so much of a driver. He couldn't see well at night."

"And he wouldn't let you drive?" Mason asked.

"No. He said he must go alone; that Julia's letter insisted he must be alone and that no one must follow him, otherwise he'd have his trip for nothing."

"Where is this note?"

"I think Grandfather put it in his coat pocket."

"Go ahead. . . . No, wait a minute. He told you he was going to *his* yacht?"

"That's what I understood him to say; that Julia wanted to meet him aboard the yacht."

"All right. Go ahead."

"Well, he went out of the garage and I went back to the house, and there was Janice, all dressed and waiting for me."

"What did *she* want?" Mason asked.

"She said she'd heard the commotion and thought perhaps there was something wrong and wanted to know . . ."

"Wait a minute," Mason interrupted. "*How* was she dressed—in evening clothes, or what?"

"No, she had on a sport outfit."

"Go on," Mason said.

"She wanted to know what had happened, and I told her. She was furious with me for letting Grandfather go, and said I should have stopped him."

"Then what?"

"Then I told her she was crazy; that I couldn't have held him with a block and tackle, and I went upstairs. I waited for her to come up. I heard her come up just behind me, and then, after a minute or two, I heard her leave her room and start downstairs again. So I sneaked out in the hall and took a look down the stairs. She was tiptoeing so as not to make any noise, and she was wearing a rain coat."

"What sort of a rain coat?" Mason asked tonelessly.

"A very light yellow rain coat."

Mason pulled a cigarette from his pocket and lit it silently. "Go on," he said.

"She sneaked downstairs," Brownley said, "and I followed her."

"Trying not to make any noise?"

"Yes, of course."

"Go on."

"She went to the garage and took out her car."

"What sort of a car?"

"A light yellow Cadillac coupe."

Mason settled back against the cushions. "You saw her leave?"

"Yes."

"How long after your grandfather left?"

"Just a minute or two."

"All right, what did *you* do?"

"I waited until she'd left the garage and then I sprinted for my car and got it started. I didn't turn on the lights, and followed her."

"Could you keep her car in sight?"

"Yes."

"You had told her your grandfather was going down to his yacht to meet Julia?"

"Yes."

"And she went down to the beach?" Mason asked.

"I don't know. That's what I wanted to tell you about."

"But I thought you said you'd followed her!"

"I did, as well as I could."

"Go ahead," Mason told him. "Tell me in your own way just what happened, but tell it to me fast. It may be important as hell."

"She was driving like the devil," Brownley said, "and it was raining pitchforks. I had to keep my lights out, and it was all I could do to follow her. . . ."

"Skip all that," Mason told him. "You followed her, did you?"

"Yes."

"Okay. Where did she go?"

"She went down Figueroa to Fifty-second Street, and then she turned off and parked the car."

"On Figueroa, or on Fifty-second?"

"On Fifty-second."

"What did you do?"

"Slid my car into the curb on Figueroa, switched off the ignition and jumped out."

"And of course that's on the road to the beach," Mason commented musingly.

Brownley nodded.

"Go on," Mason told him impatiently. "What happened?"

"She was walking ahead of me in the rain. In fact, she was running."

"Could you see her?"

"Yes. The light yellow rain coat showed up as a light patch, I ran as hard as I could without making any noise, and of course, I could go faster than she could. That light-colored rain coat was easy to follow. I could see it indistinctly, but you know how it would be. . . ."

"Yes. I know," Mason said. "Where did she go?"

"She walked four blocks."

"Walked four blocks!" Mason exclaimed.

"Yes."

"Why didn't she drive?"

"I don't know."

"You mean to say she was driving a light yellow Cadillac coupe and she parked it on Fifty-second just off Figueroa and then walked four blocks through a driving rain?"

"She ran most of the way."

"I don't care whether she was running or walking. What I mean is, she left the car and went on foot?"

"Yes."

"Where did she go?"

"There's a little apartment house there. I don't think it has over eight or ten apartments in it. It's a frame house, and she went in there."

"Any lights?" Mason asked.

"Yes. There were lights on the second floor in the right-hand corner and on one side—it's only a two-story building. The shades were drawn, but I could see the light through the shades, and occasionally I could see a shadow moving across the curtains."

"You mean you stayed there and watched?"

"That's right."

"How long?"

"Until after daylight."

Mason gave a low whistle.

"I went up to look the place over," Brownley said, "and as nearly as I could figure from the mail boxes, the front apartment was in the name of Mr. and Mrs. Victor Stockton. I couldn't tell whether the side apartment which was lighted was in the name of Jerry Franks or Paul Montrose."

"And you stayed there until after daylight?"

"Yes."

"Then what happened?"

"Well, after it got light I moved farther away of course. And then I could see the back of the building as well as the front. There were a bunch of vacant lots along there and I found one where I could stay and watch."

"And it had quit raining then?"

"It was just quitting."

"Then what happened?"

"Then Janice and a short, chunky fellow, with a felt hat, came out of the place and walked rapidly down the sidewalk toward Figueroa Street. It was daylight then and I didn't dare to crowd them too closely. I waited until they'd got quite a start. You know, it wasn't bright daylight, just the gray of dawn."

"And Janice was wearing her rain coat?"

"Yes."

"The same one she had worn earlier?"

"Yes, of course."

"What did she do?"

"She and this fellow climbed in her car and turned it around and started back toward town. I made a run for my car, but by the time I got into it, started it and turned around they were far enough away to be out of sight. I stepped on the gas and finally caught up to where I could see them. I turned up the collar of my overcoat so they wouldn't recognize me, and turned on my headlights so it would be hard for them to see what the car looked like."

"But they knew, of course, you were following, after you turned your headlights on?"

"I guess so, yes. But they didn't slow down any or try to ditch me."

"There were other cars on the road?"

"Not very many. I think I met one or two, and maybe passed one. I can't be certain. I was watching Janice."

"And what did she do?"

"She drove directly to this hotel. She and this man got out. I had a chance to see him then. I think he has gray eyes and a gray mustache. He wears glasses and . . ."

"Ever see him again?" Mason asked.

"Yes. He's up there now. He went in about fifteen or twenty minutes ago."

"The same man?"

"Yes."

"You're sure?"

"Yes."

"Look here," Mason said slowly, "there was a back exit from that apartment house?"

"Yes."

"Did you watch it while you were shadowing the place?"

"No. That's what I've been trying to explain. I watched the front and that was all. After it got light enough to see, I got where I could see both front and back, but that was only a few minutes before they came out."

"And lights were on in these apartments when Janice got there?"

"Yes."

"And you stayed there all the time, watching the place?"

"Yes."

"But she might have gone in the front, out the back and then returned through the back door any time before daylight. Is that right?"

"Yes, of course she *could* have done that."

"And you think she did?"

Brownley nodded.

"What makes you think so?"

"Because she was desperate. She's an impostor. She was going to be showed up and sent to jail."

Mason said slowly, "The thing doesn't make sense."

Brownley's tone was impatient. "I'm not claiming it makes sense," he said. "I'm telling you what happened."

Mason frowned thoughtfully at the tip of his cigarette for several minutes, then slowly opened the door of the car.

"Have you told anyone about this?" he asked.

"No. Should I?"

Mason nodded and said, "Yes, you'd better tell the D.A."

"How will I get in touch with him?"

"Don't worry," Mason said grimly, "they'll get in touch with you," and slammed the door of the car shut behind him.

Chapter 12

Mason, his face wearing a worried frown, sat in the visitor's room and looked through the wire mesh to where Julia Branner sat directly across from him. A long table stretched the length of the room. Down the center of the table ran the wire mesh, separating visitors from prisoners. A jail matron stood at the far corner of the room on the jail side. On Mason's right, back of a barred partition which was between Mason and the door, two officers were on duty. Back of them was a little room containing a veritable arsenal of revolvers, tear bombs and sawed-off shotguns.

Mason tried to hold Julia Branner's eyes with his, but she kept avoiding his gaze. Mason said, "Julia, look down at my hand—not that one, the other one. Now I'm going to open that hand causally. There's something in the palm. I want you to look at it and tell me if you've ever seen it before."

Mason glanced at the matron, looked out of the corner of his eye at the two officers, slowly opened his right hand, but carefully avoided letting his own eyes drop. Julia Branner stared as though fascinated at the hand. Slowly, Mason closed it again into a fist and pounded gently on the table as though emphasizing some point. "What is it?" he asked.

"A key."

"Your key?"

"What do you mean?"

"A man by the name of Sacks," Mason said, "a private detective, is going to claim you gave him that key and . . ."

"It's a lie! I don't know any Sacks. I don't . . ."

"Wait a minute," Mason cautioned. "Not so loud. Take it easy, sister. You probably didn't know him as Sacks, and of course you didn't know he was a detective. He's a tall, broad-shouldered chap, about forty-two or forty-three, with gray eyes

126

and regular features—that is, he *did* have regular features," Mason added with a grin. "His features aren't so regular now."

"No," she said, putting her hand to her mouth, "I never saw him. I don't know him."

"Take your hand from your mouth," Mason said, "and quit lying. Is this the key to your apartment?"

"I haven't any apartment."

"You know what I mean—the one where you were living with Stella Kenwood."

"No," she said in a faint voice. "I don't think that's the key. It's a frame-up."

Mason said, "Why did you send a message to Renwold Brownley, telling him to go down to the water-front?"

"I never did."

"Don't try to pull that," he said, frowning irritably. "They can prove you did. There's a taxi driver and . . ."

"I'm not going to say anything more," she interrupted, clamping her lips together. "I'll take my medicine if I have to."

"Look here," Mason told her, "I had faith in you and I tried to help you. You're not playing fair with me. I may be able to get you out of this, but *I've* got to know just exactly what happened. Otherwise, I'm like a prize fighter going into the ring blindfolded. You mustn't tell anyone else, but you've *got* to tell me."

She shook her head.

Mason said, "I tried to give you a square deal. Now you're lying down on me."

"You don't need to handle my case," she said. "Just get out of it. It's probably the best thing for you to do."

"Thanks for the advice," Mason said sarcastically, "but you've got me in so deep I can't get out, and you know it. I don't know how much of what I've heard is true. Perhaps you didn't plan to drag me into the case and leave me holding the sack, but it sure looks as though you did. If I try to get out now, and they convict you, I'll either go up as an accessory or I'll be disbarred, and, so far as I'm concerned, it won't make a whole lot of difference which—and I *think* that's just the way you planned it. You wanted to get me in so deep I couldn't quit. I

127

started playing around the edges and got in over my head before I knew where the deep spots were. Now I've got to get *you* out in order to get *myself* out."

She kept her lips tightly compressed. Her eyes remained downcast.

"Look here," Mason told her, "the story is that you got someone to impersonate Bishop Mallory so you could talk me into taking the case. Then you were going to make a quick clean-up and get out. Now somewhere there's a *real* Bishop Mallory. You may or may not be the real Julia Branner. Janice Seaton may or may not be your real daughter, and she may or may not be Renwold Brownley's granddaughter. There are things about this case that don't look good and don't smell good, and, in addition to all of them, there's a murder to be explained and . . ."

The woman interrupted him with a half scream. She jumped to her feet, turned toward the matron and said, "Take him away! Take him away! Don't let him talk to me!"

The matron rushed toward her. One of the officers jerked out his revolver, clicked back the lock on the barred door and moved aggressively toward Perry Mason.

Mason dropped the key from his right hand into his vest pocket and got to his feet.

"What the hell's the idea?" the officer asked.

Mason shrugged his shoulders and said calmly, "You can search me. Hysterics, I guess."

The matron led Julia Branner from the room.

Mason paced the floor of his office impatiently. Della Street, worried, sat at her desk, an open notebook in front of her. Paul Drake, freshly emerged from a Turkish bath, sprawled over the leather chair. His cold had vanished, save for an occasional sniffle.

"Tell me what *you* know first," Mason said to the detective, "and then I'll tell you what *I* know."

Drake said, "The case is nutty, Perry, any way you want to look at it. I wish you'd get out of it and stay out of it. Julia Branner is a bad egg. There's no question but what she bumped him off. There's a lot of other stuff mixed in it, but I don't think it's going to do you any good. There's . . ."

"What's the other stuff?" Mason asked.

"Janice Brownley took her car out of the garage less than five minutes after the old man left," Drake said, "and young Brownley followed her out. A couple of detectives, Victor Stockton and Pete Sacks, have been handling the thing for Janice Brownley and probably for the old man. Now Janice . . ."

"Wait a minute," Mason interrupted. "We were wondering who had fallen heir to Jaxon Eaves' cut. Now why don't these two detectives fit into that picture? You told me yourself that Eaves collected a twenty-five thousand dollar bonus for finding the girl and undoubtedly had an arrangement by which he was going to get a cut out of any inheritance she received."

Drake shook his head lugubriously. "That won't do *you* any good, Perry," he said. "Let's suppose that Eaves *did* run in a ringer. Let's suppose Stockton and Sacks did inherit his interest in the case. That doesn't help you any, because Julia Branner couldn't find the real granddaughter any more than Eaves could, so she decided to run in a ringer and collect, but she got vicious about it and evidently got tied up with a gang of crooks. The theory the D.A.'s working on—and he's got some straight dope on it from someone—is that Julia decided to wait until Bishop Mallory was taking a sabbatical year where he couldn't be reached, then she was to have someone who claimed to be Bishop Mallory contact a lawyer with a build-up. She picked on you. After you'd been sold, you were to pull the chestnuts out of the fire. But she couldn't even wait for that. She bumped off Brownley to keep him from upsetting her apple cart. Remember, she hated his guts. Personally, I think the woman's a little off in the upper story. She's brooded over this thing until she's nutty, and she's just at an age when you can't tell what form her nuttiness is going to take.

"At that, these detectives took an unfair advantage. Sacks is just a big bruiser, but Stockton is deadly as hell. He's got brains, and don't ever kid yourself he hasn't. Sacks, acting under instructions from Stockton, contacted Julia and gave her a song and dance about being a torpedo who would bump off anyone so it could never be traced, and Julia fell for it hook, line, and sinker. . . . That's the story I get from the newspaper men.—And I think Jaxon Eaves used Sacks in the original substitution—getting him to pump Julia. Then afterward, when Eaves died, Sacks cut Stockton in on the deal."

"Why can't Pete Sacks be lying?" Mason asked. "If there's a big cut coming to him of the inheritance, why wouldn't he make this whole story up out of whole cloth, just so he could get Julia in bad?"

Drake shrugged his shoulders and said, "He would, but the D.A. believes he's telling the truth. Perhaps you can make a jury believe he's lying, but what's the D.A. going to be doing with you, before you get Sacks before a jury?"

"Do you know anything more about where Janice Brownley went?" Mason asked.

"She's got an air-tight alibi."

"Really air-tight, or does it just look air-tight?"

"It looks air-tight, and I think it *is* air-tight. Victor Stockton has already reported to the D.A. He says Janice telephoned him that she thought her grandfather had gone out to make some sort of a deal with Julia Branner, and she wanted to talk things over with Stockton. Stockton wanted to come to see her, but she said she was all dressed and could drive down to his place quicker, so Stockton told her to come ahead. He lived down on Fifty-second Street, and, as I told you, he's a foxy guy. He had his wife present when Janice arrived, and then he went across the hall and got a notary public out of bed and had the notary come in."

"And the notary was there all the time?"

"Yes."

"In the same room with Janice and Stockton?"

"That's my understanding."

Mason shook his head and said, "I don't like it, Paul."

"You shouldn't," Drake said grimly.

"If Bishop Mallory was the real McCoy," Mason said, "then . . ."

Della Street interrupted to say, "There's another wireless from Captain Johanson on the *Monterey*, Chief. They've found a couple of suitcases labeled '*William Mallory, Stateroom 211*,' but Stateroom 211 is taken by people who don't answer the description of William Mallory and claim they never heard of him. The suitcases contain several yards of bandage and a suit of black broadcloth, an ecclesiastical collar, and black shoes. They were delivered to Stateroom 211 together with the baggage which really belonged there."

Mason sat down at his desk and made little drumming motions with the tips of his fingers. "And *that* doesn't make sense," he said. "Suppose Bishop Mallory is a phoney. Then where is the real bishop? On the other hand, if this was the real bishop, why should he have played ring-around-the-rosy and ducked out of the picture?"

Drake shrugged his shoulders and said, "I've got one more thing on Bishop Mallory. This is a tip which Jim Pauley, the house dick at the Regal Hotel, gave me. Before we had the bishop spotted, and before our men got on the job, a man called on Mallory. His name was Edgar Cassidy. Pauley knows him. He visited the bishop in his room and was there for about half an hour."

Mason's face showed keen interest. "Good Lord, Paul," he said, "this is the break we've been looking for. Someone who knows the bishop could tell us whether . . ."

"Hold everything," Drake interrupted. "It's just a false alarm. I rushed men out to interview Cassidy. He said that a friend of his in Sydney had written him Bishop Mallory was a good scout and was going to be visiting in Los Angeles at the Regal Hotel and to do anything he could for the bishop. Cassidy's quite a yachtsman. He has a neat little job, the *Atina*, which he uses for swordfishing. He thought the bishop might like to go out, so he dropped in to get acquainted. His testimony isn't going to help you a damned bit. He said his friend had told him the bishop was an enthusiastic fisherman, but when he contacted the bishop he didn't even get to first base. The bishop apparently wasn't interested in fishing and wasn't even cordial. Cassidy was sore when he left."

Mason resumed pacing the floor. Suddenly he paused to turn to the detective. "Cassidy's a yachting enthusiast," Mason said. "Find out if Cassidy knows Bixler. When you stop to think of it, Bixler's story about walking through the rain at that hour in the morning sounds just a little bit goofy."

Drake pulled a notebook from his pocket, scribbled a note and said without enthusiasm, "Okay, I'll find that out."

"And in the meantime," Mason said significantly, "it might be a good plan if Pauley didn't say anything to the D.A.'s men about Cassidy. I don't suppose they could use Cassidy's testimony, because it's all hearsay and conclusions, but I'd just as soon the newspapers didn't get hold of it."

Drake grinned and said, "Don't worry, Perry, that's all taken care of already. Pauley's a good friend of mine, and a little salve goes a long way with him. . . . How about young Brownley? We can't find out anything about where *he* was when the murder was committed, but his car wasn't in the garage this morning."

"I've talked with him," Mason said, "and he's going to talk with the D.A. His story isn't going to hurt Janice Brownley at all, but I still think there's something phoney about that alibi, and I don't trust Stockton."

"Stockton's nobody's fool," Drake said warningly. "Don't tangle with him, Perry, unless you have to."

Mason fished in his vest pocket and pulled out a key which he tossed to the detective. "I have to," he said, "meaning that I already have. I'm in this thing up to my necktie, Paul. That key *may* fit the apartment where Julia Branner was staying, out at 214 West Beechwood. I want you to find out if it does, and I want you to find out just as fast as you can, and then go back to your office where I can get you on the telephone."

Drake stared moodily at the key and said, "How did you happen to get the key to Julia Branner's apartment, Perry?"

Della Street sucked in a quick breath and said, "Why, Chief, isn't that the key . . ."

She bit the sentence in two and lapsed into abrupt silence. Mason stared moodily at her and said, "I'm going up to the district attorney's office. These smart dicks are trying to pin something on me, and I don't like it."

Drake said warningly, "This is a hell of a time for you to be going to the district attorney's office, Perry."

"Ain't it," Mason said, and slammed the door behind him.

Chapter 13

Hamilton Burger, the district attorney, had the build of a huge bear. He was a broad-shouldered, deep-chested, thick-waisted individual with a manner of dogged determination, short, restless arms which moved with well-muscled swiftness as he made gestures. He looked across the desk at Perry Mason and said, "This is rather an unexpected pleasure." His voice showed the surprise, but not the pleasure.

Mason said, "I want to talk with you about that Branner case."

"What about it?"

"Where do I stand in it?"

"I don't know."

"A man told me today," Mason said, "that a warrant was going to be issued for my arrest."

Burger looked him squarely in the eyes and said, "I think it is, Perry."

"When?"

"Not until I've made a complete investigation."

"What's the warrant about?"

"Assault and battery, grand larceny and conspiracy."

"Want me to explain?" Mason asked.

"*You* don't have to," Burger told him. "I know pretty much what happened. You were shadowing Janice Seaton's apartment. You wanted her in the worst way. A couple of private detectives were also on her trail. She showed up and went to another apartment. The other side got there first. That didn't suit you. You busted in and tried to pull a fast one and it came to a show-down. You smashed a guy's nose, stole his evidence against Julia Branner, pulled a gun on his partner, spirited the Seaton girl out and hid her. That may be your idea of the way to win lawsuits, but it's my idea of a way to get in jail."

"Want to hear the *facts*?" Mason asked.

Burger studied Mason for a moment and said, "You know, Perry, I've always had a great deal of respect for you, but I've always known that some day your methods were going to get you in trouble. You can't pull the stuff you do and get by with it. You've been lucky as hell, but there was bound to come a day of reckoning. It looks like this was it. I'm not going to persecute you, and I'm not going to give out any information to the newspapers until I know definitely just where we stand, but I'm inclined to think you've just about finished your professional career, and it's a damned shame.

"You know, I've always had a horror of prosecuting men. I want to be certain a person's guilty before I bring him into court. You've got a wonderful mind. There are times when you've unscrambled some mighty tough cases which would otherwise have resulted in the escape of the guilty and the conviction of the innocent, but you simply won't keep within ethical limits. You won't sit in your office and practice law. You insist on going out to try and get hold of evidence, and whenever you do, you start matching wits with witnesses and pulling some pretty fast plays, altogether too damn fast."

"Finished?" Mason asked.

"No, I haven't even started."

"Then let me interrupt," Mason said, "to tell *you* something."

"Perry," Burger said, "I've fought you in court. A couple of times you've made me seem pretty damned ridiculous. If you had come to me with some of the evidence you had in those cases I'd have co-operated with you. You chose to grandstand in court. That's your privilege. Now I'm called on to prosecute you. I'm going to do my duty. I don't think I hold any malice, in fact I like you personally, but you were bound to get it sooner or later. You're a pitcher that insists on going to the well too often. Therefore, I want you to understand me when I tell you that anything you say can be used against you, and it *will* be. There's going to be nothing confidential about this interview."

"All right," Mason said. "A couple of smart dicks come snooping into your office with a lot of stuff about me, and you fall for it without even giving me a chance to explain where I stand."

"It happens," Burger said, "that one of those smart dicks, as you call them, had some very tangible and incriminating evidence involving Julia Branner. He'd communicated with me about it and was acting under my instructions."

"All right," Mason said grimly, "here are the *facts*. You were right when you said I was looking for Janice Seaton, but I didn't find Janice Seaton. I wanted to find her, and I wanted to find out who the two men were who were sticking around waiting for her to show up. They weren't your men, and they weren't mine. I took a chance that they didn't know Janice Seaton, but only had her description. Her outstanding characteristic was a bunch of red hair, so I got Della Street, my secretary, to dye her hair, show up in the Seaton girl's apartment, check out and go to another apartment, where I'd rented a place directly across the hall so I could watch the door. I'd told Della that when anyone came in she was to string them along and find out who they were and what they were after. If the party got rough, she was to blow a whistle.

"All right, Della went to this apartment. This guy Sacks busted in on her. She was going to leave the door open. Sacks locked it. I heard something which didn't sound just right and busted in the door. I was just in time to keep Sacks from murdering Della Street. He was trying to smother her. He pulled a gun on me. I took it away from him and smashed his nose."

Burger's face showed surprise. "And it wasn't Janice Seaton at all?"

"No. It was Della Street."

"Sacks claims to have had plenty of evidence against her to convict her of several felony charges. He claims he was trying to call the police and she jumped on him, that he tried to take her in custody and you busted in."

"He choked her," Mason said, "and was trying to smother her with bedclothes when I busted in the room. . . . Does that mean anything to you?"

The district attorney nodded. "Yes," he said, "it means a lot."

Mason got to his feet. "All right, I just wanted to tell you."

"That," Burger said, "doesn't explain a lot of other things."

"What, for instance?"

"I don't want to give away my case against the Branner woman," Burger said slowly, "but Sacks met her and posed as a mobster. She offered him a big reward to kill Brownley. She gave him the key to her apartment. That key was evidence. It corroborates the story Sacks told me. When you beat him up you took everything from his pocket. You had no right to do that, Perry, under any circumstances. Among several other things, you took that key. I want it."

"I haven't got it," Mason said.

"Where is it?"

"I can produce it a little later on," Mason told him. "Have you anything except the word of this man that it really is the key to Julia Branner's apartment?"

"Yes, I have," Burger said. "But when you return the key, *if it isn't the right one*, I won't have anything except *your* word that it's the same key you took from Sacks. That's going to put you in rather an embarrassing position, because Sacks swears he went up to call on Julia Branner at about three o'clock in the afternoon and used the key, and Victor Stockton was with him and corroborates everything Sacks says."

"Why did Sacks go there?"

The district attorney said, "That's part of my case. I don't intend to disclose it. I'll tell you what I'm going to do, Perry. I'm going to hold a prompt preliminary examination in the Branner case. If you want to co-operate with me in having a complete investigation of that case, you can walk into court at ten o'clock tomorrow morning and we'll start examining witnesses. If you do that I won't have any warrant issued against you or say anything about my warrant being issued until after the evidence is all in and I know more where we stand."

"That's rushing things pretty much," Mason said. Burger shrugged his shoulders. "I could demand more time than that," Mason said. Burger lit another cigarette and said nothing. "Do I understand," Mason said, "that if we *don't* go into court tomorrow morning you'll order a warrant for my arrest?"

"No," Burger said slowly, "I don't want you to put it that way. I'm not trying to force you. I'm simply telling you that I want to investigate the circumstances thoroughly before a warrant is issued. I'm offering you one way of assisting that investigation. If you don't want to take it, I'll make an independent investigation."

"And order a complaint filed and a warrant issued?" Mason asked.

"That," Burger said, "will depend on the result of the investigation."

Mason stared steadily at the district attorney and then said bitterly, "You're giving me a hell of a break! A couple of private dicks that you don't know anything about show up with a cock-and-bull story, and you swallow it hook, line and sinker. *I* tell *you* that they're crooks, that the guy tried to kill Della Street when he thought she was the Seaton girl, and you promise to 'make an investigation.' You're worked up a lot more over my busting the guy's nose than over his trying to kill Della Street."

Burger shook his head and said patiently, "You make it sound pretty bad, Perry, but that's not a fair statement."

"Why isn't it?"

"Because when you assaulted this man you took some of the evidence that I was relying on to help you get a conviction in the Branner case. Of course, it *might* have been just a coincidence, but the fact remains that these two chaps had a piece of evidence which was going to put your client in bad; and you met up with them, smashed the chap's nose and took the evidence with you. Asking me to believe that's just a coincidence is, on the face of it, a lot."

"How much value could you put on evidence like that?" Mason protested. "It would be an easy matter for those chaps to get a key to the apartment. Give me twenty-four hours and I'll get you a key to any apartment in the city."

Burger said doggedly, "That's not the point, Perry, and you know it's not the point. That key may be trivial in itself and standing by itself, but it doesn't stand by itself. It's simply one link in the chain of evidence against your client. It's all right for you to claim it's a weak link, but that doesn't explain how you happened to assault a witness and take that bit of evidence away from him. That makes it look as though you knew it was a most important bit of evidence. I'm not taking their word against yours; I'm telling you frankly that I'm going to make an investigation and I'm not going to do anything until I've concluded that investigation. But these men are asking for a warrant. The story is going to get out to the newspapers that you beat up one of them, pulled a gun on the other and stole a piece of corroborating evidence which a jury *might* regard as a *considerable* importance. If you think I'm going to sit back and take that, you're mistaken. I've told you what I was willing to do, and that's all I'm willing to do. That's absolutely definite and absolutely final. You can either accept my proposition or not, just as you see fit."

Mason pushed back his chair and said, "Let me telephone you a little later on, can I?"

"I think we can decide the matter now," Burger told him.

"I'll telephone you within ten minutes."

"Very well," Burger said.

Mason didn't offer to shake hands. He left the office, stepped into a public telephone in the corridor, called Paul Drake and said, "Paul, did you try that key?"

"Yes," Drake said. "It fits."

"You're certain?"

"Absolutely. I opened both the outer door and the apartment door. Where does that leave you, Perry?"

Mason said, "I don't know, Paul. These dicks have hypnotized Burger. That key was evidence against Julia. It was pretty weak evidence before I took it, but my grabbing it made it loom like a ferry boat in a fog. It was a tough break. I'll be seeing you." He hung up the telephone, stepped back to the district attorney's office and said to the girl at the information desk, "Please tell Mr. Burger that Perry Mason will agree to hold the preliminary examination of Julia Branner at ten o'clock tomorrow morning. We can stipulate away all the red tape."

138

Chapter 14

Judge Knox nodded to George Shoemaker, one of the most skillful of the trial deputies in the district attorney's office. "You may proceed," he said, "with the testimony in the preliminary hearing in the case of People versus Julia Branner, upon stipulation of the Defense that witnesses are now to be examined by mutual consent and that the Defense waives any question as to time."

"So stipulated," Mason said.

Shoemaker said, "We will call Carl Smith." A stockily built man in the uniform of a cab driver came forward, sheepishly held up his hand, was sworn and took the stand.

"Your name's Carl Smith, and you are now and were on the fifth day of this month a cab driver?"

"I was."

"Do you know the defendant, Julia Branner?"

The cab driver looked down at Julia Branner who sat in tight-lipped rigidity slightly behind Perry Mason. "Yes."

"When did you see her for the first time?"

"On the night of the fifth, about one o'clock in the morning. She put in a call and I answered it. She gave me a letter addressed to Renwold C. Brownley and told me to take it out to the Brownley residence. I told her it was pretty late to do anything like that and she said it was all right, Mr. Brownley would be glad to get the letter."

"Anything else?"

"That's all she told me. I took the letter out. A young man opened the door when I rang the bell at Brownley's house. I gave him the letter. He said he'd take it to Mr. Brownley. I asked him what his name was and he said . . ."

"Just a moment," Mason snapped. "I object to any

139

conversation between these two people on the ground that it is merely hearsay and not part of the *Res Gestae*."

"Sustained," Judge Knox ruled.

Shoemaker, with a triumphant smile, turned toward the courtroom and said, "If Philip Brownley is in the courtroom, will he please stand up?" Philip Brownley, looking very slender and pale in a blue serge suit, got to his feet. "Have you ever seen that man before?" Shoemaker asked the cab driver.

"Yes. He's the man I gave the note to."

"That's all," Shoemaker said.

Mason waved his hand and said, "No questions."

"Philip Brownley, will you take the stand?" Shoemaker asked.

The young man came forward and was sworn.

"Are you acquainted with Carl Smith, the witness who has just testified?"

"Yes."

"Did you see him on the morning of the fifth?"

"Yes."

"Did he give you anything?"

"Yes."

"What was it?"

"A letter addressed to my grandfather, Renwold C. Brownley."

"What did you do with it?"

"I took it immediately to my grandfather."

"Had he retired?"

"He was reading in bed. It was his custom to read until late in the evening."

"Did he open the letter while you were there?"

"Yes."

"Did you see the letter?"

"I didn't read it, but he told me what was in it."

"What did he tell you was in it?"

Mason said, "I object, your Honor, on the ground that it's not the best evidence; that it's hearsay and is incompetent, irrelevant and immaterial."

Judge Knox said, "I will sustain the objection."

140

"What," asked Shoemaker, frowning, "did your grand-father do or say immediately after receiving the letter?"

"Same objection," Mason said.

"I won't admit any statement as to what was in the letter nor whom it was from," Judge Knox ruled, "but I will admit, as part of the *Res Gestae*, any statements that might have been made by Mr. Brownley as to what he intended to do or where he intended to go."

Philip Brownley said in a low voice, "He said he had to go down to Los Angeles harbor at once to meet Julia Branner. I understood him to say he was going to meet her aboard his yacht."

"Move to strike out the part about meeting Julia Branner," Mason said, "as not responsive to question, incompetent, irrelevant, immaterial and hearsay."

"I will reserve a ruling," Judge Knox said, "but I'll leave it in if subsequent testimony shows it to be what I consider part of the *Res Gestae*."

"It's too remote to be part of the *Res Gestae*," Mason objected.

"I don't think so, Mr. Mason. However, that will depend somewhat on the evidence. You may renew your motion later on if, after the evidence is all in, it appears to be too remote."

"Did he say anything else?" Shoemaker asked.

"Yes. He said the she-devil had kept his son's watch for years and now she was willing to let it go."

"Move to strike that out," Mason said, "as not being part of the *Res Gestae* and as being an attempt to show the contents of a written document by parol; as hearsay, incompetent, irrelevant and immaterial."

"Motion is granted. It will be stricken," Judge Knox ruled. "It is not part of the *Res Gestae*."

"What did your grandfather do?" Shoemaker asked.

"He dressed, went to his car and drove out of the garage about two o'clock."

"You're acquainted with Perry Mason, the attorney who is representing the defendant?"

"Yes."

"Did you see him on that same evening, or rather on the evening of the fourth?"

"Yes. It was around eleven o'clock, between eleven o'clock and midnight."

"Did you talk with him?"

"Yes."

"Did you discuss your grandfather's will with him?"

"Yes."

"Did he discuss a conversation he had had with your grandfather?"

"In a way, yes."

Mason said, "Your Honor, I object to an attempt to prove that conversation until proof has been made of the *corpus delicti*."

Shoemaker said, "Your Honor, I'm not going any farther into the conversation at *this* time. Later on I expect to prove that Perry Mason learned on the evening of the fourth that Renwold Brownley intended to execute on the morning of the fifth documents which would transfer the bulk of his estate to his granddaughter, Janice Brownley; that Mason communicated that information to his client, and that this furnished the motive for murder. However, I am not going into it at the present time. You may cross-examine, Mr. Mason."

Mason said, "You were waiting for me when I left your grandfather's house?"

"Yes."

"How long had you been waiting?"

"Only a few minutes."

"You knew when I left the room where I had been talking with your grandfather and went to my car, didn't you?" Mason asked.

"Yes. I heard you leave the room."

"And then you went out to stand in the driveway and wait for me. Is that right?"

"Yes."

"But," Mason said, "your clothes were soaking wet. It was raining hard, but not hard enough to wet you to the skin in the few seconds which elasped between the time I left the room

142

where I was with your grandfather and the time you met me in the driveway. How do you account for that?"

Young Brownley lowered his eyes and said nothing.

"Answer the question," the Court ordered.

"I don't know," Brownley said.

"Isn't it a fact," Mason asked him, "that you had been standing out in the rain *before* I left the house? Isn't it a fact that you could hear much, if not all, of what was said in my interview with your grandfather? Weren't you listening outside one of the windows?"

Brownley hesitated. "You answer that question," Mason thundered, getting to his feet, "and tell the truth."

"Yes," young Brownley said after a moment, "I stood outside of the window and *tried* to hear what was being said. I couldn't hear it all, but I heard some of it."

"So," Mason said, "you knew then that your grandfather was going to execute these documents in the morning, documents which would irrevocably place the bulk of his estate in the hands of the young woman who was living there in the house as Janice Brownley."

"Yes," Philip Brownley said slowly.

"So," Mason went on, "so far as motive is concerned, *you* had a motive for murdering your grandfather. In other words, you stood to profit by his death. If he died before those documents were executed, your inheritance would have been one-half of the estate, in the event Janice Brownley was *really* a granddaughter. And if it could be proved that she was *not* the granddaughter, your inheritance would have been the *entire* estate. Is that right?"

Shoemaker jumped to his feet. "Your Honor," he shouted, "I object! The question is argumentative, irrelevant, incompetent and immaterial. It's not proper cross-examination. It calls for a conclusion of the witness upon matters of law."

"I am asking it," Mason said, "only to show bias on the part of the witness."

"I think," Judge Knox ruled, "that the question is argumentative and calls for a conclusion. If you want to prove it, you'll have to do it by asking the witness how much of the conversation was heard, just what was said, and leave the legal effect of it for the Court to determine.''

Mason shrugged his shoulders and said, "I have no further questions of the witness.''

Shoemaker hesitated as though debating the advisability of asking further questions on re-direct, then shook his head and said, "The witness is excused. Call Gordon Bixler.''

Gordon Bixler, a bony-faced individual of about forty-five, wearing a gray business suit, took the witness stand and testified that his name was Gordon Bixler; that he was a yachtsman, was the owner of the yacht *Resolute*; that on the night of the murder he had been on a trip to Catalina in his yacht; that he had returned in a driving rain and had telephoned from the clubhouse for his Filipino boy to meet him with a car; that he had then attended to certain details in connection with the mooring of his yacht and leaving it in condition for the next cruise; that his Filipino boy had not shown up; that he had waited for more than an hour and had heard an automobile in the road near the clubhouse; that he had gone out to investigate, thinking his Filipino boy had become confused, since he had only been at the Yacht Club on one previous occasion; that he had started walking toward the headlights of the automobile whose motor he had heard, and had observed that the car was being driven very slowly; that, while he was watching it, a woman who wore a white rain coat walked out from the side of the road; that the car stopped and the young woman stepped to the running board, and spoke for a few moments to the driver of the car; and thereupon the woman stepped back to the ground and the car ran slowly on down the road and had almost reached the witness when it turned into a side street, over to another road, speeded up, turned and circled back; that it had almost reached its original position when he saw the young woman in the white rain coat step out from the shadows, and jump to the running board of the car; that by this time the witness thought his Filipino boy had had trouble of some sort and thought that he might be able to get the man in the car to give him a lift; that he started walking toward the car and suddenly saw several stabbing flashes and heard the rapid reports of a gun; that he thought there were five shots in all, but there might have been six; that he saw the woman in the white coat jump from the running board and run to the shadows. A Chevrolet automobile, which had been parked in the shadows of a crossroad, roared into motion and swept down the road away from him at high speed. The witness ran to the other automobile. A man's body was lying with the left arm and shoulder and the head hung over the left-hand door of the car. Blood was running from bullet wounds down the outside of the car and collecting in a pool on the left-hand running board. The man was Renwold C. Brownley and was dead. The witness had met Brownley on several occasions, and there was no chance he could be mistaken.

The witness then admitted that he became rattled and confused; that he ran blindly through the rain until he encountered a car driven by some man whom he did not know, but who had later turned out to be Harry Coulter, a private detective; that in company with this detective, the witness searched for the Brownley car and failed to find it; that they had telephoned officers, who had finally arrived and taken up the search; that the time, as nearly as he could fix it, when the shooting took place was about two forty-five in the morning; that he had telephoned for officers about ten or fifteen minutes past three o'clock.

Shoemaker turned the witness over to Mason for cross-examination.

"You were badly rattled?" Mason asked.

"I was, yes, sir. It was all so sudden and so unexpected that I became very much confused."

"Why didn't you get into Brownley's car and drive it and him to the nearest hospital?"

"I just never thought of it, that's all. When I saw this dead man sprawled out with his head and shoulders hanging over the window, and realized it was Renwold Brownley and that he'd been murdered, I became confused."

"And you were pretty much confused *before* you recognized Brownley, weren't you? The knowledge that this woman in the white rain coat had fired several shots at close range at the driver of that car had naturally upset you, hadn't it?"

"Yes, sir, it had."

Mason placed the tips of his fingers together and took his eyes from the witness to stare intently at his fingertips. "It was raining?" he asked.

"Yes."

"Raining hard?"

"Well, it wasn't raining quite as hard then as it had been a little while before. There had been a let-up; but it was raining."

"This was near a yacht club of which you are a member?"

"Yes."

"There's a fence separating that yacht club from the highway?"

"Yes."

"No street lights?"

"No."

"It wasn't moonlight?"

"No, sir."

"No stars visible?"

"No, sir. . . . I see what you're getting at, Mr. Mason, but there was plenty of light to enable me to see what I've testified to."

"What was the source of that light?"

"There's a mast in front of the clubhouse of the yacht club and there are flood-lights on this mast to illuminate the moorings and the parking spaces where members keep their cars."

"And how far were those flood-lights from the place where the crime was committed?" Mason asked.

"Perhaps three or four hundred feet."

"So that this road was brightly lighted?"

"No, sir. I didn't say that."

"But it was lighted?"

"There was some light."

"Enough to enable you to see objects distinctly."

"Understand, Mr. Mason," Bixler said with the belligerent manner of one who had been carefully coached to avoid a certain trap, "this woman wore a white rain coat which made her quite visible after she stepped out of the shadows. The road was dark, all right, and there were deep black shadows, but

146

when the woman stepped to the running board of the car there was enough illumination so I could see her figure quite distinctly. I couldn't see her features and I haven't tried to identify her."

"Your identification," Mason asked, "is due to the fact that she wore a white rain coat. Is that right?"

"Yes."

"How do you know it was white?"

"I could see it was white."

"Couldn't it have been a light pink?" Mason asked.

"No."

"Or a light blue?"

"No."

Mason suddenly raised his eyes from his fingertips to stare intently at the witness. "Are you willing to swear," he asked, "that it was not a light *yellow*?"

The witness hesitated, then said, "No. It wasn't a light yellow."

"Didn't have *any* yellow in it?" Mason asked.

"No, sir."

Mason said slowly, "You understand, there's a distinction between pure white and a light buff, or a cream color?"

"Yes, sir, of course."

"And sometimes, even in daylight, it's difficult to distinguish these colors?"

"Not particularly. I know white when I see it. This was a white rain coat."

"For instance, this sheet of cardboad," Mason said, whipping an oblong of pasteboard from his pocket, "is it white or yellow?"

"It's white."

Mason took another sheet of dead-white cardboard from his pocket, held it up, side by side with the other, and a titter ran through the courtroom.

Bixler said hastily, "That's my mistake, Mr. Mason. That first piece of cardboard had *some* yellow coloring in it. It looked white because you were holding it up against your dark suit. But, now I see the white cardboard placed beside it, I can see the difference in color."

Mason said casually, and after the manner of one who is seeking to help a witness clarify his testimony, "And if a white sheet had been held back of that rain coat you saw the night of the murder it would have helped you to detect the light yellow tint in the rain coat, just in the same way this white card has enabled you to see the difference between it and the yellow card. Is that right?"

"Yes, sir," the witness said, then lowered his eyes and said, "I mean, no, sir. That is, I *think* it was a white rain coat."

"But it *might* have been a light yellow one?" Mason asked, gesturing with the hand which held the two pieces of cardboard so that the witness's eyes shifted to the pieces of cardboard.

Bixler glanced helplessly at the deputy district attorney, at the unsympathetic faces of spectators in the courtroom. He slumped within his clothes as though his self-assurance had been suddenly deflated. "Yes," he said, "it *might* have been a light yellow rain coat."

Mason got slowly and impressively to his feet. Staring steadily at the confused witness, he said, "How did you know Brownley was dead?"

"I could tell by looking at him."

"You're positive?"

"Yes, sir."

"But you were badly rattled at the time?"

"Well, yes."

"And you didn't feel for his pulse?"

"No, sir."

"You could only see him in the illumination which came from the dash light of the automobile?"

"Yes, sir."

"You've never studied medicine?"

"No, sir."

"How many dead people have you ever seen in your life—I mean before they were embalmed and placed in coffins?"

The witness hesitated and said, "Four."

"Had any of those persons died by violence?"

"No, sir."

"So this was your first experience in viewing a man who had been shot, is that right?"

"Yes, sir."

"And yet you're willing to swear the man was dead when you made no examination?"

"Well, if he wasn't dead he was certainly dying. Blood was spurting from those wounds."

"Ah," Mason said, "he might have been dying, but not dead."

"Well, perhaps."

"And when you say that he was dying, you don't claim to have any medical skill, and had never before seen any man who was dying from gunshot wounds?"

"No, sir."

"And had never seen a man die from gunshot wounds?"

"No, sir."

"But you do know generally that sometimes men are shot, sometimes seriously, and ultimately recover, don't you?"

"Well . . . yes. I've heard of such cases."

"Now, do you want to swear that this man was dying?"

"Well, I *thought* he was dying."

"You wouldn't think much of a doctor who took a look at a man in the dim light given by the dash light of an automobile and then turned away and said the man was dead or dying and nothing could be done for him, would you?"

"No, sir."

"You'd expect a doctor to listen for heart action with a stethoscope, wouldn't you?"

"Yes, sir."

"Yet *you* expect to look at the *first* man you had ever seen shot and be able to tell more than a trained physician, who had handled hundreds of similar cases, and without making the examination the physician would have had to make in order to reach an opinion?"

"Well, no, sir, I wouldn't say that."

"Well, then, you don't know the man was dying, do you?"

"Well, I knew he had been shot."

"Exactly," Mason said, "and that's *all* you know, isn't it?"

"Well, he was lying there all slumped over in a heap and he'd been shot, and there was blood on his head and on his clothes."

"Exactly," Mason said, "that's all you can swear to. You heard shots fired, ran to the car, saw a man slumped over and bleeding, and that's all you know, isn't it?"

"Yes, I guess so."

"You don't know whether he was dead?"

"No."

"Nor whether he was dying?"

"No."

"Nor whether the shots were more than mere flesh wounds."

"Well . . . no, I didn't examine him."

"That," Mason said, "is all."

"No re-direct," Shoemaker said, hesitating a moment.

"Call your next witness," Judge Knox ordered.

Shoemaker called the police officers who had answered the telephone call to the harbor. They testified to the search they had made for the automobile, of finally discovering bloodstains on the pavement; of tracing the reddish stains, which had been mixed in with the rain water, until they came to a pier; that they had grappled and had pulled an automobile to the surface; that the car was that of Renwold C. Brownley; that it had been left in low gear and was still in low gear when recovered; that the hand throttle had been pulled open and that, after the car had been recovered, tests made with it showed that the position of the hand throttle was such that the car would go exactly 12.8 miles per hour in low gear with the hand throttle in the same position as when the car had been recovered; that they had found a .32 caliber Colt automatic on the floor of the car; that they had found some empty cartridges; that they had recovered from the upholstering of the car two bullets, one of which had evidently missed the occupant of the car, the other showing evidences of having passed through human flesh.

At this point, Judge Knox announced that the hour was twelve-thirty, and adjourned court until two o'clock in the afternoon.

Mason, Della Street, and Paul Drake went to lunch in a little restaurant on North Broadway, where they were able to secure a booth.

"What do you make of it, Paul?" Mason asked.

"You going to make a fight on the question of *corpus delicti*?"

"Yes. I had been hoping I could do it all along. But I wasn't certain what Bixler would testify to. I was afraid he might swear positively the man was dead, and stick to it. As it is, I think I can get the case thrown out of court."

Drake nodded. "You made a swell job of that cross-examination, Perry. Bixler was so rattled Shoemaker was afraid to try any re-direct."

"Isn't that going to be a highly technical defense?" Della Street asked.

Mason said grimly, "You're damned right it's going to be a technical defense. But, nevertheless, that's the law. Many people have been hanged on circumstantial evidence, where it subsequently appeared that the supposed victim never had been killed, but was alive and well. And that's the reason they made the law the way it is. The term, *corpus delicti*, means the body of the Offense. In order to show it, in a charge of homicide, the Prosecution must show death as the *result*, and the criminal agency of the defendant as the *means*. Now the Prosecution's going to run up against one big hurdle on this *corpus delicti* business. They can't show death, and if they're not careful, I can trap them into being crucified by their own proof."

"How do you mean?" Della Street asked.

"It's a goofy crime," Mason said. "The woman, whoever she was, fired the shots from the automatic, and then beat it. Now, the evidence shows that she beat it in her own car, going at high speed. *Someone* drove Brownley's car into the bay. That someone couldn't have been the person who did the shooting, because she had been seen by the Prosecution's own witness dashing madly away from the scene of the crime. It's improbable that she had a confederate who remained in the background while the shooting took place, only to step out subsequently and drive the car off the end of the wharf.

"The only other explanation is that Brownley was unconscious when Bixler looked in the car; but that after Bixler left, Brownley recovered consciousness enough to try to drive the car in search of help; that he managed to get the car started, but was driving more or less blindly through a lashing rain, became confused on roads, and drove himself off the end of the pier."

Drake nodded slowly.

"Now, then," Mason said, "*if* when they recover Brownley's body, they find he died of drowning, it doesn't make any difference whether he *might* have died of the gunshot wounds within the next thirty minutes or the next thirty seconds. The fact that his death occurred from drowning, rather than from the wounds, means they can't convict Julia Branner of murder, because the wounds weren't the actual cause of death. That's a technical point, but it's been adjudicated."

Della Street frowned at her coffee cup and said, "Listen, Chief, on all your other cases you've been representing someone who was innocent. You've managed to bring the case to a spectacular conclusion by showing that the Prosecution had made a bad guess. People are for you. You have a reputation now, both as a lawyer and a detective; but the minute you resort to the ordinary tactics of the average criminal lawyer, you're going to turn people against you. If you use your ingenuity to get a guilty woman acquitted on a technicality, people are going to think you are tied up with murderers. They're going to lose their respect for you."

Mason said slowly, "In other cases, Della, I was more or less in the clear. On this case I'm in up to my necktie. They're going to put Pete Sacks on the stand. The minute they do that, and he testifies that Julia Branner asked him to murder Brownley and gave him the key to her apartment, and then says that I trapped him into a position where I stole that key from him, it's going to look like hell. That key wouldn't have been important if I hadn't taken it—but when I grabbed it, I made it the most important bit of evidence in the case. If the district attorney overlooks it, the Bar Association won't."

"Could you keep Sacks from testifying if you tripped them up on this *corpus delicti* business?" Drake asked.

"That's exactly the point," Mason told him. "That's why I'm making this defense. If I can beat the case on the *corpus delicti*, I'll get Julia Branner off temporarily. They'll throw this case out of court and everything will then wait until they recover Brownley's body. Sacks will never get a chance to tell his story, and the key won't seem so important. When they do find the body, the chances are I can prove Brownley died by drowning. *Then*, if the district attorney proceeds against me, it'll look like spite work. I've *got* to beat them on this *corpus delicti* angle. And after I do that, I've got to find more facts that will help our theory of the case."

The detective said, "I've got men working on every angle of the case, Perry, but I can't find out a damn thing that's going to help us any. I've traced Mallory from the time he left the steamship in San Francisco until he arrived in Los Angeles. He stayed at the Palace Hotel in San Francisco, went directly there from the ship, and as nearly as the hotel employees in San Francisco can tell, the bishop who checked out was the same bishop who checked in."

"That bishop," Mason said, drumming with his fingertips on the edge of the table cloth, "in some way is the key to the whole business. Why did he call on me? Why did he disappear? If he's the real goods, why did he take a runout powder? If he's an impostor, why didn't he pull a more convincing fade-out . . . telephone me he had to leave on a secret mission and ask me to carry on? There were plenty of ways he could have kept up the pretense, yet eased himself out of the picture. The darn case is driving me nuts because I can't get a toe-hold. I'm clawing at a blank wall. And why does Julia Branner act the way she does? Why won't she talk to me? Can't she see she's sending herself to the gallows and putting me in an impossible position?"

"Perhaps she won't talk because she's guilty," Della Street suggested.

"I'm not so certain she's guilty," Mason remarked. "The theory of the crime the Prosecution has worked out doesn't sound any too logical. She *may* be protecting someone else and *may* be innocent, herself."

Drake said, "Forget it, Perry. How in hell could anyone have framed this crime on her? *She* wrote the note to Brownley.

When they find his body they'll find the note in his pocket. It will be in her handwriting. It will crucify her. She lured him down to that place near the waterfront. There's no possibility of doubt on that score. She wanted him killed, both for her daughter's sake, and because she hated him. How could anyone have taken *her* gun without her knowing it, have gone to the very place where she instructed Brownley to be, dressed in exactly the same clothes, and driving the same make of car? Remember, Julia Branner didn't write that note until *after* you'd telephoned her and told her what was in the wind. Therefore, her whole scheme of luring Brownley to the waterfront was hatched after that time; and anyone who wanted to frame her must necessarily have started from scratch after that note was written. I tell you, it's impossible."

Mason looked at his watch and said, "Well, we'll go back to court and see what develops. We're not licked yet by a long ways."

"If Pete Sacks ever takes the stand and swears you framed him and stole that key from him, it doesn't make much difference what happens after that. Public sentiment will have turned definitely against you," Drake said. "You've *got* to keep him from telling his story, either by this *corpus delicti* defense or in some other way."

Mason shrugged his shoulders.

Della Street said, softly, "Listen, Chief, you put *me* on the stand and let me tell *my* story. Do it just as soon as you can after Sacks tells *his* story. I'll fix him. I'll tell what he tried to do to me, and, after that, people will want to lynch him. And if Shoemaker wants to try to rattle me on cross-examination I'll do plenty to him."

Mason squeezed her hand and said, "Good girl. I know I can depend on you."

As they left the restaurant, Drake said to Mason in a low tone, "You can't let her do that, Perry. It'll look as though you two trapped Sacks, that Della led him on by luring him to her apartment. It looks too damned much like a badger game. It'll put Della in a hell of a position before the public."

Mason said gloomily in the same low, growling tone of

voice, "Do you think *you're* telling *me* anything? But don't let her know. I'm not even going to put her on the stand."

Della Street said, "What are you two getting your heads together about? You sound as though you were hatching up some deviltry. Come on or you'll be late for court."

Chapter 15

Shoemaker put witnesses on the stand in rapid succession, after the manner of a prize fighter who is facing a groggy opponent and is anxious to press the advantage. A ballistics expert testified the bullets found in the car had been fired from the .32 automatic found on the floor of the car. A hardware dealer from Salt Lake produced records showing that Julia Branner had purchased the automatic from him. An officer on the Salt Lake police force showed that Julia Branner's permit to carry a weapon described the same automatic and gave the number which appeared on the gun. A fingerprint expert testified that after the car had been pulled from the water it had been dried and an attempt made to develop latent fingerprints; that on the upper edge of the glass on the left-hand door, a fingerprint had been discovered which coincided with the middle finger on the left hand of the defendant.

Shoemaker rose to his feet, said dramatically, "Call Peter Sacks to the stand."

Sacks, his nose and cheeks completely concealed by a smear of bandages and strips of adhesive tape, came forward and was sworn.

"Do you know the defendant, Julia Branner?" Shoemaker asked, after Sacks had testified to his name, age, and address.

"Yes," Sacks said in a thick voice.

"Did you ever have any conversation with her in which she mentioned Renwold Brownley?"

"Yes."

"Do you know Perry Mason, the attorney who is representing her?"

"Yes."

"When you had your conversation with Julia Branner who was present?"

"Victor Stockton."

"Anyone else?"

"No."

"Where did the conversation take place?"

"At the United Airport at Burbank."

"What's your occupation?"

"I'm a private detective."

"Had you had any previous correspondence with the defendant in this case?"

"Yes, sir."

"During that conversation, had you posed as being a certain type of person?"

"Yes, sir. I'd posed as a mobster and boasted of the murders I'd committed for money."

"What was the date of the conversation you are testifying about, at which Mr. Stockton was present?"

"On the fourth day of this month."

"At what hour?"

"About ten o'clock in the morning."

"Now what was said, and by whom was it said?"

Mason got to his feet and said, "Your Honor, it now appears that the Prosecution are seeking to link the defendant with the crime of murder, yet the Prosecution have failed to establish any murder. I object to the question on the ground that it is incompetent, irrelevant, and immaterial; that no proper foundation has been laid; that it is not part of the *Res Gestae*, and no part of the *corpus delicti*; that the Prosecution, to date, have signally failed to prove the *corpus delicti*."

"We don't have to prove it as we would in a Superior Court," Shoemaker interposed. "This is only a preliminary. We only have to prove that a crime has been committed and that there's reasonable cause to believe the defendant committed it."

"Nevertheless," Mason said, "you can't prove murder in *any* court without proving the *corpus delicti*. Now, according to the Prosecution's own theory, someone, *other than the defendant*, must have driven Renwold C. Brownley's automobile from the place where the shooting occurred, to the wharf. The defendant had gone, if we are to believe the

157

testimony of Mr. Bixler. Now, what is more reasonable than to suppose that Mr. Brownley, himself, recovered consciousness, started to drive the car, became confused in the rain, and drove it off the end of the wharf? In that event, he would have met his death by drowning, and not from gunshot wounds. And, in order to prove murder, the Prosecution must prove death as a direct result of the act of the defendant.''

"Not at all," Shoemaker argued vehemently. "If, your Honor, Counselor's contention is correct and Mr. Brownley *did* die of drowning, the drowning would have been caused by the unlawful acts of the defendant, to wit, the shooting which incapacitated him from driving his car intelligently.''

"But," Mason said, "you haven't proved that the shooting incapacitated him from driving the car. You haven't proved how many times he was shot, whether any of the shots were in a fatal place, or whether they were merely flesh wounds. The gun was a small caliber gun and it's very possible the bullets followed around under the skin without penetrating any vital organs. Moreover, if this man met his death by drowning, unless the defendant, or some accomplice drove that car off the end of the pier, the defendant certainly can't be held responsible for a death by drowning. The minute you concede there's even a possibility Brownley recovered consciousness and drove that automobile into the bay, you have made a stronger argument against your case than anything I can say. You, yourself, tacitly admit that you aren't convinced by the evidence you yourself have produced!''

Shoemaker's face flushed. "This," he roared, "is an attempt to thwart justice by a technicality which . . .''

"Just a moment," Judge Knox interrupted, "the Court has been giving this matter some thought, ever since it noticed the remarkably ingenious cross-examination of the witness Bixler. There's some question here as to the means of death. There's even some question as to whether death itself has been proved. It is reasonable to suppose that Renwold Brownley was in the automobile when it went over the edge of the wharf, but there's not evidence indicating that such was the case. I am fully aware that the degree of proof required to bind the defendant over is not the same as that required in a Superior Court upon a trial of the issues on the merits; but I am also aware that if I should dismiss this case at the present time, the defendant will not have been in jeopardy and therefore can again be re-arrested when the body of Renwold Brownley is discovered. I think you will admit, Mr. Deputy District Attorney, that you would hardly care to prosecute this defendant in a Superior Court upon a charge of murder, until after the body itself has been discovered."

"That's not the point," Shoemaker said, very evidently keeping his temper by an effort. "This is only a preliminary. We want to get the defendant bound over. We want to get the evidence in such shape we know where we stand. And there are other reasons why we are particularly anxious at this time to get the evidence of these witnesses before the public . . . that is, before the Court."

Mason shrugged and said, "Counsel's tongue slipped. He *meant* before the public."

Knox frowned and said, "That will do, Mr. Mason. You will refrain from making any such comments and confine yourself to the question under discussion." He glowered at Mason for a moment, then turned hastily away to keep from smiling.

Shoemaker, so indignant as to be speechless for the moment, stood groping for words with which to clothe an effective argument.

"I'm going to adjourn this case until tomorrow morning at ten o'clock," Judge Knox said. "At that time, Counsel can argue the question; but I am very much inclined to hold that at the present time the *corpus delicti* has not been shown, and while perhaps technically I should confine myself only to a question of whether a crime has been committed, I'm inclined to take a broader view of the situation, particularly because a dismissal of the case at this time would not be a bar to a subsequent prosecution."

"But," Shoemaker protested, "would your Honor claim that we haven't shown a sufficient case of assault with a deadly weapon?"

Judge Knox smiled and said, "And would the district attorney's office be willing to have the Court bind over the defendant only on a charge of assault with a deadly weapon with intent to commit murder and release her from a murder charge?"

"No!" Shoemaker shouted. "We're going to prosecute her for murder. That's what she's guilty of. . . ." As he realized the full effect of his statement, he let his voice drop into a low tone, hesitated for a moment, then sat down uncertainly.

Judge Knox let his smile become a grin. "I think, Counselor," he said, "your own argument illustrates better than anything I could say the fallacy of your present contention. Court will take a recess until tomorrow morning at ten o'clock. The defendant is, of course, remanded to the custody of the sheriff."

Perry Mason glanced over his shoulder at Paul Drake. The detective had produced a handkerchief from his pocket and was mopping his forehead. Mason himself heaved a sigh of relief as Judge Knox arose from the bench. Turning to Julia Branner, Mason said, "Julia, won't you please tell me . . ."

Her lips clamped in a thin line. She shook her head, arose from the chair and nodded to the deputy sheriff who was waiting to take her back to the jail.

Chapter 16

Della Street twisted her fingers around Perry Mason's right hand, where it rested on the steering wheel and said, "Chief, isn't there something I can do? Couldn't I go talk with the district attorney?"

He shook his head, keeping his eyes on the road.

"Couldn't I take the rap? Couldn't I say that I took the stuff, that I took the key?"

"No," he said, "Burger's after me. He doesn't think he's holding any malice, but, for a long time now, he's been predicting that I'd come a cropper. Naturally, he's prejudiced in favor of making his predictions come true."

"Chief," she said, snuggling close to him, "you know I'd do anything, *anything*."

Mason kept his left hand on the steering wheel, slipped his right hand about her shoulders, squeezed her affectionately. "Good kid, Della," he said, "but there's nothing you can do. We've just got to take it."

"Listen, Chief," she said, "how *was* that crime committed? It doesn't sound reasonable that the district attorney's theory is right."

"Julia *might* have done the shooting in a wild blaze of temper," he admitted, "but in that case there'd have been some sort of an argument first. She didn't lure him down there to kill him, that's a cinch. Otherwise, she wouldn't have left so broad a back trail."

"Then why *did* she lure him down there?"

"That's something I can't tell you," he said, "but it has something to do with our stuttering bishop, our disappearing Janice Seaton, and perhaps a few others."

"And she didn't intend to kill him when she left the apartment?"

"Not one chance in a hundred," Mason said.

"But didn't you tell me that when you went there in the morning Stella Kenwood had been sitting up all night, that her attitude showed she knew Julia Branner had gone out to do something that was going to get her into trouble if she was caught?"

Mason suddenly slammed the brakes on the car, skidded into the curb, kicked out the gear lever and stared at Della Street with wide eyes. "Now," he said, "you're talking."

"What do you mean, Chief? You mean . . . ?"

"Wait a minute," he said, "I want to think." He sat there in the car, the motor running, traffic streaming past. Once or twice he nodded his head. Then he said, "Della, it's so damned wild that it doesn't sound logical, but it's absolutely the only thing which will explain the facts in this case, and, when you stop to think of it, it's so absolutely plain and open that the great wonder is we didn't realize it before. Have you got your shorthand notebook with you?"

She opened her purse and nodded her head.

Mason slammed home the gear shift lever, kicked in the clutch. "Come on," he said, "we'll go places." He swung the car out from the curb and made time to the frame apartment house on Beechwood, rang Stella Kenwood's bell, received an answering buzz which released the catch on the door. "Come on, Della," he said, "we'll go up. When we get in that room, pull out your notebook and take down everything that's said and don't lose your head, no matter what happens."

They climbed the stairs and walked down the corridor to Stella Kenwood's apartment. Mason knocked on the door. Stella Kenwood opened it, peered at him with a white, anxious face, blinked her faded, watery eyes, and said in a thin, expressionless voice, "Oh, it's you."

Mason nodded.

"Come in," she said.

"My secretary, Miss Street."

"Yes, I saw her in court today. What does it mean, Mr. Mason? Aren't they going to take any evidence against Julia?"

Mason said, "Sit down, Mrs. Kenwood. I want to ask you some questions."

162

"Yes," she said tonelessly, "what?"

Mason said, "Your daughter has been in an automobile accident. I want you to prepare yourself for a shock."

Her mouth sagged open. Her eyes grew wide.

"My daughter?" she asked.

"Yes."

"But I haven't any daughter . . . she's dead. She died two years ago."

Mason shook his head and said, "I'm sorry, but it all came out. She's dying and she wants you to come to her. She made a complete confession."

The woman sat perfectly still, staring at Mason with her tired eyes, her white face apathetic and hopeless. Finally she said in a tired voice, "I knew something like this would happen. Where is she?"

"Get your hat," Mason said, "we'll go to her. How long had you been planning on the substitution, Stella?"

"I don't know," she said in that same lifeless voice, "ever since Julia told me about her daughter, I guess. I realized what a chance there'd be for some girl."

"So you got in touch with Mr. Sacks?"

"Yes. He was a detective in Salt Lake."

"And he worked through Jaxon Eaves here?"

"That's right. Tell me, how did the accident happen?"

"A crash at a crossing," Mason said. "Come on, we'll have to hurry to get there in time."

The woman buttoned a faded blue coat with threadbare elbows about her thin frame. Mason said to Della Street, "Get District Attorney Burger on the line and tell him to meet me in the reception room of the Good Samaritan Hospital. Read him this conversation over the telephone. Tell him to burn up the road getting there."

Stella Kenwood said, "He won't try to make things hard for my daughter now, will he? If it's the end, he won't trouble her with a lot of questions, will he?"

"I don't think so," Mason said. "Come on, let's go."

He left Della Street in the apartment while he escorted Stella Kenwood down the stairs and into his car. He raced the car into speed, said to Stella Kenwood, "I'm afraid you'll have to make a complete statement to the district attorney in order to get him to let you be with her at the last."

"There's no hope?" she asked.

"None whatever," Mason told her.

"I'm sorry," she said. "I tried to do what was best, but somehow I knew it was going to work out all wrong, and then when it looked as though we were going to be exposed . . ."

Mason roared the car into speed.

"Yes?" he prompted. "When it looked as though you were going to be exposed, then what?"

She took a handkerchief from her purse, sobbed into it quietly, nor would she answer any more questions.

Mason looked at his wristwatch from time to time, drove his car frantically through traffic. He skidded to a stop in front of the Good Samaritan Hospital, helped Stella Kenwood from the car. They walked up the stairs through an entrance door and into a reception room. Hamilton Burger, his face wearing a puzzled frown, arose to meet them. A man with a shorthand notebook open in front of him sat at a table. He did not look up as they entered.

Perry Mason said, "Stella, you know the district attorney?"

"Yes, he questioned me the day they took Julia to jail."

Mason turned to the district attorney. "Burger," he said, "this is the end. Stella Kenwood's daughter is dying. We want to get all of the preliminaries over with as soon as possible so Stella can be with her daughter. Perhaps I can save time if I give you the highlights of the story as her daughter told it to me. Then Stella can confirm it and you can let her go in to the bedside.

"Stella Kenwood had a daughter about the same age as Julia Branner's daughter. Julia Branner had an apartment with Stella in Salt Lake and told Stella her history. Stella realized what a wonderful chance there'd be to get her daughter a home with a millionaire if she could convince Brownley that her daughter was his granddaughter. She talked with Peter Sacks, who was a private detective in Salt Lake. He got in touch with Jaxon Eaves. The less said about their methods, the better, but because Stella had secured all of the facts and all of the little incidental details from Julia, she managed to make a build-up which completely fooled Brownley. And so Stella Kenwood's daughter became Janice Brownley, and Julia knew nothing whatever about it. As Janice Brownley, the Kenwood girl won Brownley's confidence, became a favorite, was in line for an enormous inheritance.

"Then she went to Sydney, Australia, returned on the *Monterey*, going, of course, under the name of Janice Brownley, granddaughter of Renwold C. Brownley. Bishop William Mallory was a passenger on that boat, and Bishop Mallory hadn't forgotten. He asked questions, and, in a panic, the girl realized that her answers were inadequate and that Mallory suspected the truth. She wirelessed her mother, and her mother appealed to Sacks, who was now living in Los Angeles, where he could protect his 'interests.'

"Stella was anxious to keep Julia from finding out about it. You see, they'd persuaded Renwold Brownley that it would be very poor business to permit any publicity when the girl came to live with them, so it was all handled very quietly. Sacks, of course, was frightened because he thought the bishop might go directly to Brownley.

"But the bishop did a little wirelessing on his own account, definitely ascertained that the girl he had met on the boat was an impostor and then wired Julia Branner to meet him in Los Angeles, and, in Los Angeles, Bishop Mallory also found Janice Seaton, the real grandchild. From a letter received from an attorney who was probating the estate of the last of Janice's adopted parents, Bishop Mallory learned there was no longer any need to keep the pledge of secrecy he had given when the girl was adopted. Furthermore, the bishop received evidence indicating to him that when Seaton lay dying, realizing his own financial affairs had become so hopelessly involved he couldn't leave the girl any substantial amount of property, he had tried to get a message to Bishop Mallory asking the bishop to disclose the girl's real identity. Seaton was too far gone to make his message clear to those who were listening; but he said enough so the bishop knew what was wanted and decided to act accordingly.

"When Julia showed up, Stella was frantic. She got in touch

with Sacks. Sacks realized he had to get the real granddaughter out of the way if he could.

"This is right, is it, Mrs. Kenwood?"

She nodded her head and said in a low voice, "Yes, that's right as far as I know. You know more about the bishop than I do. But the rest of it's right. Go ahead, let's get it over with."

Mason said, "They were frantic. Sacks was willing to go to any lengths, even murder, and then Julia threw Stella into a panic by announcing she was writing a note to get Brownley to meet her down at the harbor, where she was going to show him his real granddaughter. You see, Janice Seaton had grown to look very much like her father. Julia had seen her that afternoon, and felt that if Brownley could see her he'd recognized the family resemblance right away. She knew she had one sure way of luring Brownley to a rendezvous with her, and that was Oscar Brownley's watch, the one Renwold had given him. Renwold wanted that watch very, very badly.

"Stella knew that would be the end of everything. The conspiracy would be discovered. She didn't care for herself, but it would mean jail for her daughter. She was desperate, so she slipped the gun from Julia's purse. She told Julia to take her Chevrolet and she borrowed or rented another Chevrolet. Julia was wearing a white rain coat. Stella dressed herself in a white rain coat. She raced down to the beach and actually beat Julia there, but her plan almost went astray when Julia showed up before Brownley. In fact, Julia was the one who first climbed on the running board of Brownley's car. That's when Julia left the fingerprint on the window of the coupe. But Stella hadn't given up hope. Julia had intended to have Brownley drive slowly around a bit so that she could see he wasn't followed. Stella knew that, and she decided to take a chance. She kept hidden while Brownley drove in a big loop around a couple of the streets, then ran out from the shadows and beckoned to Brownley. Brownley naturally stopped the car. Stella jumped to the running board, fired five shots from Julia's automatic, dropped it inside the car, raced for her machine and drove away.

"In the meantime, Julia, as soon as she heard the shots, had run to her own car; but she didn't get it started for a few minutes. Stella beat Julia home, undressed, and waited for her. Julia was so excited she didn't go directly back to the apartment, but drove around for a while, calming her nerves."

Mason turned to Stella Kenwood and said, "*That's* right, Stella, isn't it?"

"Yes," she said, "that's right."

"And that key Sacks had," Mason said, "was the key to the apartment, all right, but *Stella* had given it to him instead of *Julia*. *That's* right, isn't it, Stella?"

"That's right," she said, "but my daughter doesn't know anything about my shooting Brownley. No one knows anything about that. I would have told Pete Sacks what I intended to do, if I could have got him on the telephone, but I couldn't. When I knew what Julia intended to do, I just couldn't see my daughter go to jail. I didn't intend to frame the crime on Julia— not at first. I just wanted a gun and I didn't have one, so I took the one out of Julia's purse. But how could my daughter have confessed all this to you, Mr. Mason, when she didn't know it herself?"

Mason said, "I'm sorry, Stella. I had to trap you into a confession."

"How much of this did my daughter tell you?"

"None of it."

"Then she isn't . . . isn't? . . ."

Mason shook his head and said, "No, Stella, she isn't hurt. I had to do it this way in order to right a wrong. It was the only way I could think of."

Stella Kenwood slumped wearily in her chair, then started to cry. "It's a judgement," she said. "I guess I couldn't have gone through with it anyway. I wish you gentlemen could see my side of it . . . life always so hard. . . . I was fighting for my daughter. I didn't care for myself . . . here was this opportunity going to waste. Julia wouldn't let Brownley have her daughter, and Brownley wanted a granddaughter, so I gave him one. . . . And then the bishop showed up, and Pete Sacks told me we'd all go to jail. I didn't care for myself. It was for my daughter. I'm willing to die. Go ahead and let the law kill me, but please don't be too hard on my girl. She did it because her mother told her to."

A nurse entered the room and said to Hamilton Burger, "Mr. Burger, your office wants you on the telephone."

"Not now," Burger said, his eyes on Stella Kenwood. "Tell them I can't be interrupted. There are one or two matters I want to clean up here before . . ."

The nurse said, "They said I was to tell you it was *very* important; that it was a new development in the Brownley matter."

Burger frowned thoughtfully. "I can plug a phone in here," the nurse said.

Burger nodded to the nurse, turned to Stella Kenwood and said, "Are you going to make a written statement, Stella?"

She said, "Why not? I've told you everything, and I feel better. I'm a wicked woman, but I don't want my daughter to suffer."

The nurse brought a desk telephone, plugged it in and handed it to Burger, who said, "Hello," and then frowned thoughtfully as he listened for several seconds. He glanced significantly at Perry Mason and said, "Leave things just as they are. Don't touch anything. Get Philip Brownley and Janice Brownley to make the identification; but don't let them see it until I get there. Have a shorthand reporter on the job. You'll have to stall things along for a few minutes because I can't get away from here for ten or fifteen minutes yet. I'm getting a written statement." He hung up the telephone, caught the significance of Mason's lifted eyebrows and nodded his head. "Yes," he said, "found just a few minutes ago."

Stella Kenwood, her chin sunk on her chest, had apparently paid no attention to the conversation.

Chapter 17

The speedometer needle of Mason's car quivered at around seventy miles an hour. Della Street, in the front seat beside him, lit a cigarette with the electric lighter, took it from between her lips and proffered it to Mason.

"No, thanks, Della," he said, "I'll drive now and smoke afterwards."

Paul Drake, in the back seat, yelled, "Take it slow, Perry. There's a curve ahead."

Mason said grimly, "When *you* were at the wheel, you looped the loop on this curve and thought it was funny. Now I'm driving, and you'll take it and like it."

The car screamed into the curve, lurched, straightened, skidded and then, as Mason depressed the foot throttle to the floorboards, came out of the turn and into the straightaway. Drake heaved a sigh of relief and let go his hold of the robe rail. Della Street, exhaling cigarette smoke, said, "Do they know whether he died from drowning or from the gunshot wounds, Chief?"

"If they know, they aren't saying," he told her. "It'll probably take a fairly complete post-mortem to tell."

"And you've already pointed out to them what they're up against," she said. "If he died by drowning, they can't convict Stella Kenwood of murder. Just what could they do to her?"

"Prosecute her for assault with a deadly weapon with intent to commit murder. However, having guessed wrong on the crime the first time they made a pass at it, it isn't going to be so easy to get a conviction in front of a jury. Burger will realize that, so he'll move heaven and earth to make a perfect case now."

"And *if* he died of the gunshot wounds?" she asked.

"That'll make a murder case out of it," Mason said, "only

then they've got to prove how the car happened to be driven over the edge of the wharf, and that's not going to be so easy, because, regardless of what the autopsy surgeons say, if Renwold Brownley was able to drive the car off the wharf, a jury won't think he was dead when he went over the edge. And there'll be a lot of sympathy with Stella Kenwood. Then, if Brownley was killed by the bullets, someone must have driven the car over. That someone would have been an accomplice."

"Of course," Della Street pointed out, "he *could* have recovered consciousness and started to drive the car. He could have put it into low gear and, in a half-conscious condition, driven along the pier thinking it was a road. Then he could have died with the car still in gear, and the weight of his body depressing the foot throttle . . ."

Mason interrupted with a laugh and said, "That's something that *could* have happened. Remember that a district attorney has to prove to a jury beyond all reasonable doubt what actually *did* happen."

Drake yelled, "For God's sake, Della, quit talking so much and let him drive the car. That truck almost sideswiped us! It was the hand throttle which sent the car over the pier. You're a swell secretary, but don't try to make a detective out of yourself, because women can't develop the type of minds detectives need to have—and don't distract Mason's attention with a lot of arguments, or we'll all be corpses!"

Della said, "It's your cold that makes you such a grouch, Paul. Don't think just because you're a man, God gave you a corner on detective ability."

"That isn't what I meant," Drake explained. "I don't want to argue it now; but being a detective means you have to remember thousands of details and automatically fit any theory into the facts. You illustrated the point just now by forgetting about that hand throttle."

Mason grinned and said, "Don't argue with him, Della. He's got a cold and he's full of dope, fever and egotism."

Della Street lapsed into frowning silence. Drake closed his eyes. Mason, devoting his entire attention to driving the car, sent the speedometer needle shivering upward.

"Did Mr. Burger arrange to have *both* Janice Brownley and

Philip Brownley come down to identify the body?" she asked at length.

Mason nodded.

"Why?" she wanted to know.

Mason said, "We'll know more about that when we get there. Incidentally, Paul, I'm getting a theory about this case. It's never going to be really solved until we've found out about that stuttering bishop. Is Harry Coulter going to be there?"

"Yes. He got the flash, and should be there before we arrive, or get there right afterwards."

"I want him to look over that car of Janice Brownley's," Mason said. "It's a yellow Cadillac. I want him to see if there's anything about it he can recognize."

Drake nodded, and Mason slowed as he approached the more congested district of the harbor.

"Her alibi's pretty air-tight," Drake pointed out, as Mason made a boulevard stop. "Paul Montrose has a pretty good reputation. He's a notary public working in a real estate office. He swears that Stockton got him out of bed to come in and join the party."

"*Why* did he do that?" Mason asked, throwing the car into second and stepping on the throttle.

"Because Stockton wanted some disinterested witness to back up his testimony."

"He had his wife," Della volunteered.

"Yes, but he wanted someone else," Drake said wearily.

"And," Mason said, frowning, "this was *before* Janice arrived, wasn't it?"

"Yes, about five minutes before, according to Montrose's statement."

"Well, we'll see what we'll see," Mason said, swinging the car to the right. "Hello, there are a lot of cars here."

"Mostly news photographers," Drake said. "Wait a minute, this cop is going to stop us."

A uniformed policeman stepped out, held up his hand and said, "You can't go out on the pier, boys."

While Mason hesitated, Drake, with the ready wit of a detective who has had to resort to extemporaneous prevarications on numerous occasions to crash police lines, pointed to

Della Street and said, "We've got to go there. This is Janice Brownley. District Attorney Burger told her to get here just as fast as she could to identify the body of her grandfather."

"That's different," the officer admitted. "I had instructions about her, but I thought she was already there."

Drake shook his head and said, "Drive on, Perry. Be brave, Janice. It'll soon be over."

Della Street dabbed at her eyes with her handkerchief, and the officer stood to one side.

"Suppose Harry Coulter could get through all right?" Mason asked.

"Sure," Drake said, "it's a cinch. He probably couldn't get his car through, but you can leave it to Harry to think up some excuse which will get him past a cop who's as dumb as that one."

Mason said, "There's a yellow Cad coupe over there, Perry. Let's park in close to it, give it a once-over and see if it's Janice's car."

Mason swung his car in close to the big yellow coupe. Drake jumped from the rear seat, walked boldly to the side of the coupe, flung open the door, looked at the registration certificate and said, "Okay, Perry, it's her car."

Mason said, "There may be some distinguishing mark on it that Coulter might have remembered, perhaps a dented fender or . . . Hello, what's this?" He paused to look at a dent in the left front fender. "This has been done recently," he said.

"It's just a fender dent which might have been done in a parking lot," Drake observed, coming to stare at the fender.

Della Street, looking over the leather upholstery in the car, called out excitedly, "Chief, look here!"

They hurried back to join her, and she pointed out several reddish-brown spots on the deep leather-covered shelf which was just back of the front seat. For a moment the three of them stood staring at the stains. Drake said, "You've got a good eye, Della. Those things are all but invisible against this russet leather."

She grinned and said, "Just the feminine ability to observe things, Paul. A man wouldn't see them."

172

"And that's why they were overlooked," Mason said.

"Do you suppose Janice could have been at the beach and loaded her grandfather's body into the car and. . . . ?"

"Not much chance," Mason said. "Let's get away from here. Those bloodstains are evidence. They've been overlooked. If anyone knows we've discovered them, the stains will be removed before we can prove their significance."

"But what are they evidence of?" Drake asked.

"We'll figure that out later," Mason said.

They walked down the pier some twenty yards to where an ambulance had been drawn up. A group of men with cameras and flash bulbs were taking close-ups of Philip Brownley and Janice Brownley. Hamilton Burger nodded to Perry Mason. "It's the body all right?" Mason asked.

"Yes, it's Renwold C. Brownley. The body evidently spilled out of the car, and the tide washed it back under the pier."

"Did he die by drowning or by gunshot wounds?" Mason asked.

Burger shook his head.

"Can't tell or won't?" Mason asked.

"I'm not making any statements right now," Burger announced.

Mason looked over toward the ambulance. "May I see the body?"

"I think not, Perry. Julia Branner's out of it. You're not going to defend Stella Kenwood, are you?"

"No, one client in a case is enough for me."

Drake muttered in Mason's ear, "There's Harry Coulter. I'll get him to take a look at that yellow Cad."

Burger turned away, and Mason said, "Have him do his looking from a distance, Paul. Let's not show that we're taking any interest in that car. I want to figure out those bloodstains before we do anything more."

As Drake moved away, Philip Brownley came up to Mason and said, "Horrible, isn't it?"

Mason stared at him steadily. "No more horrible than it has been all along, is it?"

Young Brownley gave a visible shudder. "Finding Grandfather's body this way brings the tragedy of it all home to me so forcibly."

"You saw the body?"

"Yes, of course. I had to identify it."

"How was he dressed?"

"Just as he left the house."

"How about the pockets of the coat, any documents?"

"Yes, there were some papers. They were pretty badly water-soaked. The police took them."

"Did you get to see them?"

"No, the police were very secretive about it. . . . Tell me, Mr. Mason, you intimated when you were cross-examining me that if Grandfather didn't leave a will, and Janice *isn't* the granddaughter, I'd inherit the entire estate. Is that the law?"

Mason, staring at him steadily, said, "You'd like to squeeze Janice out of it, wouldn't you?"

"I'm just asking you what the law is. You know how I feel about her. She's an adventuress."

"I think," Mason told him, "you'd better consult a lawyer yourself. I don't want you for a client."

"Why not?"

Mason shrugged his shoulders and said, "I might want to take an adverse position."

"You mean representing Janice?"

"Not necessarily," Mason said.

"What *do* you mean then?"

"Figure it out," Mason told him.

The clanging gong of the ambulance called for the right of way. The car purred into slow motion, then, as it cleared the crowd, moved into greater speed. Drake took a few steps toward Perry Mason and nodded his head significantly. Mason moved over to join him.

"Harry says it looks like the car," Drake said, "but there are no distinguishing marks on it that he could remember well enough to swear to in court. If it isn't the car he saw, it's almost a dead ringer for it."

"And it was parked down near the place where Renwold Brownley kept his yacht?"

"Yes."

Mason touched Drake's arm and pointed across to where some yachts were moored. "Take a look, Paul," he said, "isn't the name on that yacht the *Atina*?"

Drake squinted his eyes and said, "It looks like it to me, Perry."

Della Street said positively, "Yes, that's the *Atina*."

"That's the yacht owned by the Cassidy who called on Bishop Mallory?"

Drake nodded.

Mason said, "Della and I are going places. I've got a hunch, Paul. Suppose you and Harry go take a look aboard the yacht."

"What for?" Drake asked.

"For anything you may happen to find," Mason said slowly.

"We may have some trouble getting aboard. There's a watchman, and it's a private mooring."

Mason said irritably, "For the love of Mike, do I have to tell you how to run a detective agency?"

"No, you don't," Drake drawled. "All I'm trying to find out is how strong we should go. How important is it that we get aboard that yacht?"

Mason, squinting his eyes against the sunlight which was reflected from the water of the bay, said, "Paul, I think it's damned important. You and Harry get aboard that yacht."

"That's all we wanted to know," Drake said. "Come on, Harry."

Mason motioned to Della Street. "Come on, Della," he told her, "we've got a job."

"What sort of a job, Chief?" she asked.

"Checking the records of receiving hospitals," he told her. "Let's go."

Della Street emerged from the telephone booth with a list of names. "These are the emergency cases you wanted to know about," she said, "together with the outcome. Numbers three, four and ten are dead. They were all identified. Number two is the only one who's still unconscious and unidentified."

Mason took the list, nodded and said, "Come on, we're going places." He snapped on the ignition, slammed the car into gear and started driving at high speed back towards Los Angeles.

"What did you think Drake was going to find aboard the *Atina*?" Della Street asked.

"Frankly," he told her, "I don't know."

"Why didn't you stay to find out?"

"Because," he said, "I doped out a theory of the case which may hold water."

"What is it?"

"I'll tell you," he said, "when I see whether it checks out. In solving a crime, a man has to figure out lots of theories. Some of them hold water, and some of them don't. A man who wants to build up a reputation for himself will keep his thoughts to himself until he knows that they check out."

Her eyes were tender as she studied his profile. "Do you want to build up a reputation for yourself, Chief?" she asked softly.

"And how!" he told her. They made the rest of the trip in silence. Mason brought the car to a stop before a hospital. Together they entered the office, and Mason said, "We want to look at the man who was picked up with a fractured skull on the morning of the fifth."

"He's not allowed visitors and . . ."

"I think," Mason said, "we can identify him."

"Very well. One of the internes will permit you to enter the room. He's still unconscious. You'll have to promise to remain absolutely silent." Mason nodded. The girl pressed a bell and said to a white-robed interne who appeared, "Please take these parties to 236. It's a matter of identification. They've promised to remain silent."

They followed the interne down a corridor and into a ward past long rows of beds to a cot which was in a corner hidden by screens from the rest of the ward. The interne folded back one of the screens. Della Street gasped, and her hand shot to her throat.

Mason stared down at the unconscious figure, then nodded to the interne, who replaced the screen. Mason pulled a roll of bills from his pocket. "See that this man has the best medical attention money can buy," Mason said. "Transfer him to a private room and give him a day and a night nurse."

"You know him?" the interne asked curiously.

Mason nodded and said, "The man is Bishop William Mallory of Sydney, Australia."

Chapter 18

Mason sat in the swivel chair behind his office desk, body tilted back, feet propped on the edge of the desk, ankles crossed. He was smoking a cigarette, and a satisfied smile played around the corners of his lips.

Della Street, perched informally on the corner of the desk, grinned across at him and said, "All right, Mr. Human Enigma, what's the theory? It's held water, so kick through and tell me what it is. Don't be such a tightwad. How did you know that was Bishop Mallory, and what did you expect Drake was going to find aboard the *Atina*?"

Mason studied the twisting smoke from his cigarette for a few seconds, then began to speak in a low, meditative voice. "Julia didn't intend to kill Brownley, but she *did* want him to go down to the beach. Therefore, there was something she expected to do when he was at the beach, something which was important enough so that some other people were willing to kill Brownley in order to keep him from doing it.

"Now there's only one answer, only one logical conclusion. Janice Seaton looked enough like the dead Oscar Brownley so that the minute Renwold clapped eyes on her he'd know she was Oscar's daughter, and, since Oscar only had one daughter, that would put the fake Janice Brownley out on the end of a limb. So, naturally, when Stella realized that Julia Branner had some hold by which she could make Renwold Brownley go to the beach, and knew that while he was at the beach he was going to be confronted with his real granddaughter, whose features would be unmistakable proof of her identity, Stella was faced with a show-down. She didn't care on her account. What she did was done through mother-love, a warped mentality, and because of a situation a couple of crooks had engineered her into. She had a rain coat which was very similar

178

to that worn by Julia Branner, which was probably a coincidence, because she didn't intend to be seen, but she did intend to kill Renwold Brownley with Julia's gun, so she loaned Julia her car and then made arrangements to get another.

"Now then, look at the case from the other end. Julia evidently knew that the matured Janice Seaton was the spitting image of Oscar Brownley. This was one bit of irrefutable proof none of us had taken into consideration. But *how* did Julia know it? The only way she could possibly have known it is that she *must* have seen Janice arriving here from Salt Lake City. Since only Bishop Mallory knew the whereabouts of the real Janice, it follows, therefore, that Mallory must have met her and brought mother and child together before Julia Branner came to my office and before Drake's men got on the job shadowing Mallory at the Regal Hotel.

"Now then, Julia wanted Renwold to go to the beach. She was going to meet him. She was going to take him to Janice Seaton, and she intended at that time to furnish Brownley with unmistakable proof of Janice Seaton's relationship to him. Therefore she must have intended, first, to show him the family resemblance, and, second, to confront him with Bishop Mallory. Therefore Bishop Mallory was to be someplace at the beach; but Bishop Mallory knew he was being followed, knew that an attempt had been made on his life and doubtless surmised that the people he was fighting would be only too willing to murder Janice Seaton if they could locate her, so Bishop Mallory went to the beach *and disappeared*. He used the *Monterey* as a means of disappearance. He might have chosen any one of a dozen different stepping stones toward invisibility. The reason he chose the *Monterey* was because it was conveniently located. Therefore, he must have arranged for a hiding place near the waterfront, and he had been called on earlier in the day by Cassidy, who was the owner of the *Atina*.

"What's more reasonable than to suppose that Bishop Mallory and Janice were waiting for Julia and Renwold Brownley aboard the *Atina*? The bishop was smart enough to know that the other side would kill Janice if they had a chance, and therefore Julia had insisted that Renwold Brownley was to come alone. She was to meet him at a spot close enough to enable her to take him at once to the *Atina*, yet far enough removed from the place of concealment so the other side wouldn't know where Janice was hidden, if Brownley should mention where he was going.

"Now notice the peculiar series of events which are so closely interwoven that they fairly scream at the real solution. Stella Kenwood started out on her own, determined to kill Renwold Brownley, but she says her daughter wasn't to know anything about it, because she didn't want to involve her daughter in murder. She was making a mother's sacrifice. Philip Brownley talked with his grandfather just before Renwold left for the beach. Renwold Brownley told Philip generally what was in the note, and said he was to meet Julia Branner and go aboard *a* yacht. Philip Brownley didn't hear him clearly, because as soon as he heard the word 'beach' and 'yacht' the association of ideas made him think at once of his grandfather's yacht which was moored at the beach, so young Brownley reported to the fake granddaughter that Renwold had gone down to meet Julia aboard his yacht, and the fake Janice reported over the telephone to Victor Stockton, who must have arranged at once to kill Brownley and to get an ironclad alibi for Janice, who would be a logical suspect. Now why does a man arrange an alibi in advance?"

Mason paused to peer steadily at Della, who, with a little gasp, said, "Why, because he knows he's going to need one."

"Exactly," Mason said. "In other words, the minute Victor Stockton went to such elaborate pains to give Janice Brownley an alibi, it was because *he knew she was going to need one*. Therefore, *he* knew that Renwold Brownley was going to be murdered, but he didn't know Stella Kenwood had already arranged for the murder, because Stella wasn't going to let her daughter know anything about it.

"Therefore Stockton worked out a swell scheme for a murder. Janice was to come to his house, but leave her car parked some four blocks from his place. She probably didn't know what Stockton had in mind. Stockton's accomplice could then take Janice's car to the beach to lie in wait for Renwold. Renwold would recognize Janice's car. He had unlimited confidence in Janice and would unhesitatingly approach the car, to be met with a fusillade of shots which would kill both Julia and Renwold Brownley. So Peter Sacks picked up Janice's car as soon as she left it. He rushed to Brownley's yacht, intending to kill Brownley and, perhaps, Julia Branner. Now Sacks had received his information through Stockton, who, in turn, had received it from Janice, who thought Renwold was going to *his* yacht instead of to another yacht.

"Therefore, at the time of the murder, we have Julia Branner waiting at the beach to make certain Renwold was driving alone and was not followed. We have Stella, who had arrived on the scene first, determined to kill Brownley. We have Peter Sacks waiting in Janice Brownley's automobile in front of Renwold Brownley's yacht, and we have Bishop Mallory and Janice Seaton waiting aboard the *Atina*, which was also moored in the yacht basin.

"When Stella pulled the trigger of the automatic, the shots were plainly audible to both Sacks and the bishop. Both must have realized what those shots might mean. Harry Coulter was driving a car, and the sound of his motor and the rain on the roof kept him from hearing the shots. Bishop Mallory didn't have a car, so he started for the scene of the shooting on foot. Sacks started in Janice Brownley's car and therefore was the first to arrive. He saw what had happened, probably made a closer examination than Bixler had and saw Brownley wasn't dead. He slid into Brownley's car, threw it into gear, ran it to the nearest pier, pointed it for the bay, left it in low gear and opened the hand throttle. Then he went back to Janice's car and started to drive away, only to encounter Bishop Mallory running toward the scene of the shots. Sacks recognized the bishop, swung the car toward him and smacked the bishop down, fracturing his skull and probably thinking he'd killed him. But he didn't want Bishop Mallory found there, so he loaded him into the car, carried him to the outskirts of Los Angeles and then dumped him out, after first removing all evidence of the bishop's identity and . . ."

Mason was interrupted by Paul Drake's code knock on the door. "All right, Della," he said, "let's see what Drake's uncovered."

Della started to the door, paused halfway to say, "But why wouldn't Julia Branner have talked, and why wouldn't Janice Seaton . . . ?"

"Because," Mason said, "Julia Branner thought Bishop Mallory and her daughter were keeping quiet because of some very important reason. She wasn't going to say a word until she knew where they stood. Janice Seaton knew that Bishop Mallory had placed her aboard the yacht telling her not to move from it until she heard from him. She probably thought there had been some trouble in getting Renwold Brownley to come down to the yacht. Unless I miss my guess badly, she doesn't even know anything about the murder."

Della Street nodded, opened the door. Drake burst excitedly into the office and said, "You'll never guess what we found aboard that yacht, Perry—not in a hundred years! We found . . ."

Della Street interrupted him to say, "Janice Seaton, still waiting for Bishop Mallory to return. She didn't even know Renwold had been murdered."

Drake stared at her with his mouth sagging open. "How the hell did *you* know?" he asked.

Della Street closed her right eye in a surreptitious wink at Perry Mason. "Elementary, my dear Watson," she said, "elementary. My feminine mind reasoned it out from the facts of the case."

Drake sat down weakly in the nearest chair. "I," he announced, "will be damned."

Chapter 19

It was noon of the next day that Mason hung up the telephone, nodded to Della Street and said, "The autopsy shows he met his death by drowning."

"Where does that put everyone?" she asked.

"It makes Stella Kenwood guilty of a technical assault with a deadly weapon. It makes Peter Sacks and Victor Stockton guilty of first degree murder. The autopsy shows Brownley would probably have bled to death from a bullet wound which had severed one of his large arteries, but it also shows unmistakably that his death was actually caused by drowning."

"Can the district attorney prove the conspiracy between Sacks and Stockton?"

Mason grinned and said, "That's up to him. I'm not running the district attorney's office, but I think he can. Stockton left himself wide open when he arranged such an elaborate alibi for Janice before he had any reason to believe Brownley was going to be murdered."

"I take it," she said slowly, "that in the future Burger won't be so quick to issue warrants for your arrest."

Mason grinned and said, "As a matter of fact, Burger has asked me if I'll have dinner with him this evening. He wants to 'talk over the case.' Now that Bishop Mallory's regained consciousness and is going to live, Burger's got a pretty good case. I drove over to the hospital this morning to see the bishop. Mallory remembers seeing the yellow coupe, saw it swerve and deliberately drive into him. That, of course, is the last he remembers, but with the dent on the fender and human bloodstains on the back of the seat, Burger's got a pretty good case of circumstantial evidence. And remember, these men are rats. They'll turn on each other when it comes to a show-down, particularly if the D.A. can make Sacks think Stockton deliberately engineered it so he'd be in the clear and Sacks would climb the thirteen steps to the gallows."

"It all clicks, Chief," said Della slowly. "But there's one thing that still puzzles me. If the bishop is a real bishop, and not a phoney, what about that stutter?"

Mason grinned. "I thought of that myself," he said. "I asked Mallory about it this morning. He told me all about it: It seems that when he was a boy, he used to stutter. He cured himself of the habit, but every time he got an emotional shock, the stutter would come back to him. When he met the false Janice Brownley on the ship, and realized that she was a fake, and that his promise to Charles Seaton kept him from exposing a serious crime, he was so upset that he began stuttering again. He was still suffering from that shock when he came into my office."

About the Author

Erle Stanley Gardner is the king of American mystery fiction. A criminal lawyer, he filled his mystery masterpieces with intricate, fascinating, ever-twisting plots. Challenging, clever, and full of surprises, these are whodunits in the best tradition. During his lifetime, Erle Stanley Gardner wrote 146 books, 85 of which feature Perry Mason.